Sara looked at Gabe, lifting her chin as she met his gaze.

"Please summon your men, Mr. Porter. I need to brief them, and tell them how I wish to proceed with the mission."

"Yes, ma'am," he said, grinning and saluting her. "Anything you say, ma'am. You're the boss of this outfit." He turned and strode from the room.

You've got that straight, buster, Sara thought with a decisive nod. The first order she issued ought to be that Gabriel Porter was not allowed to smile that knock-'em-dead smile. Lord, the man even had a dimple in his right cheek. Not fair, not fair at all.

Forget it, Sara, she told herself in the next instant. The important thing was the mission at hand. They would find the missing men and bring them home, alive and well. Everything would be fine.

It just had to be.

Dear Reader,

Welcome to Silhouette Special Edition...welcome to romance.

That telltale sign of falling leaves signals that autumn has arrived and so have heartwarming books to take you into the season.

Two exciting series from veteran authors continue in the month of September. Christine Rimmer's THE JONES GANG returns with *A Home for the Hunter*. And the Rogue River is once again the exciting setting for Laurie Paige's WILD RIVER series in *A River To Cross*.

This month, our THAT SPECIAL WOMAN! is Anna Louise Perkins, a courageous woman who rises to the challenge of bringing love and happiness to the man of her dreams. You'll meet her in award-winning author Sherryl Woods's *The Parson's Waiting*.

Also in September, don't miss *Rancher's Heaven* from Robin Elliott, *Miracle Child* by Kayla Daniels and *Family Connections*, a debut book in Silhouette Special Edition by author Judith Yates.

I hope you enjoy this book, and all of the stories to come!

Sincerely,

Tara Gavin
Senior Editor

Please address questions and book requests to:
Silhouette Reader Service
U.S.: 3010 Walden Ave., P.O. Box 1325, Buffalo, NY 14269
Canadian: P.O. Box 609, Fort Erie, Ont. L2A 5X3

ROBIN ELLIOTT
RANCHER'S HEAVEN

Silhouette®

SPECIAL EDITION®

Published by Silhouette Books
America's Publisher of Contemporary Romance

If you purchased this book without a cover you should be aware that this book is stolen property. It was reported as "unsold and destroyed" to the publisher, and neither the author nor the publisher has received any payment for this "stripped book."

This book is dedicated to the volunteers who make up the Yavapai County Sheriff's Office Search and Rescue Response Team Back Country Unit.
Gentlemen, with appreciation and admiration, I salute you.
I would like to express my heartfelt gratitude to Yavapai County Back Country Unit team member Bob Turner, who spent countless hours providing me with the information I needed regarding Search and Rescue procedures, equipment and attitudes.
Without Bob's assistance, this book never would have been possible.
Any errors are mine.
Thank you, Thirty-three-oh-six, from One-oh-one. Over and out.

SILHOUETTE BOOKS

ISBN 0-373-09909-6

RANCHER'S HEAVEN

Copyright © 1994 by Joan Elliott Pickart

All rights reserved. Except for use in any review, the reproduction or utilization of this work in whole or in part in any form by any electronic, mechanical or other means, now known or hereafter invented, including xerography, photocopying and recording, or in any information storage or retrieval system, is forbidden without the written permission of the editorial office, Silhouette Books, 300 East 42nd Street, New York, NY 10017 U.S.A.

All characters in this book have no existence outside the imagination of the author and have no relation whatsoever to anyone bearing the same name or names. They are not even distantly inspired by any individual known or unknown to the author, and all incidents are pure invention.

This edition published by arrangement with Harlequin Enterprises B.V.

® and TM are trademarks of Harlequin Enterprises B. V., used under license. Trademarks indicated with ® are registered in the United States Patent and Trademark Office, the Canadian Trade Marks Office and in other countries.

Printed in U.S.A.

Books by Robin Elliott

Silhouette Special Edition

Rancher's Heaven #909

Silhouette Intimate Moments

Gauntlet Run #206

Silhouette Desire

Call It Love #213
To Have It All #237
Picture of Love #261
Pennies in the Fountain #275
Dawn's Gift #303
Brooke's Chance #323
Betting Man #344
Silver Sands #362
Lost and Found #384
Out of the Cold #440
Sophie's Attic #725
Not Just Another Perfect Wife #818
Haven's Call #859

ROBIN ELLIOTT

lives in a small, charming town in the high pine country of Arizona. She enjoys watching football, attending craft shows on the town square and gardening. Robin has published over sixty novels and also writes under her own name, Joan Elliott Pickart.

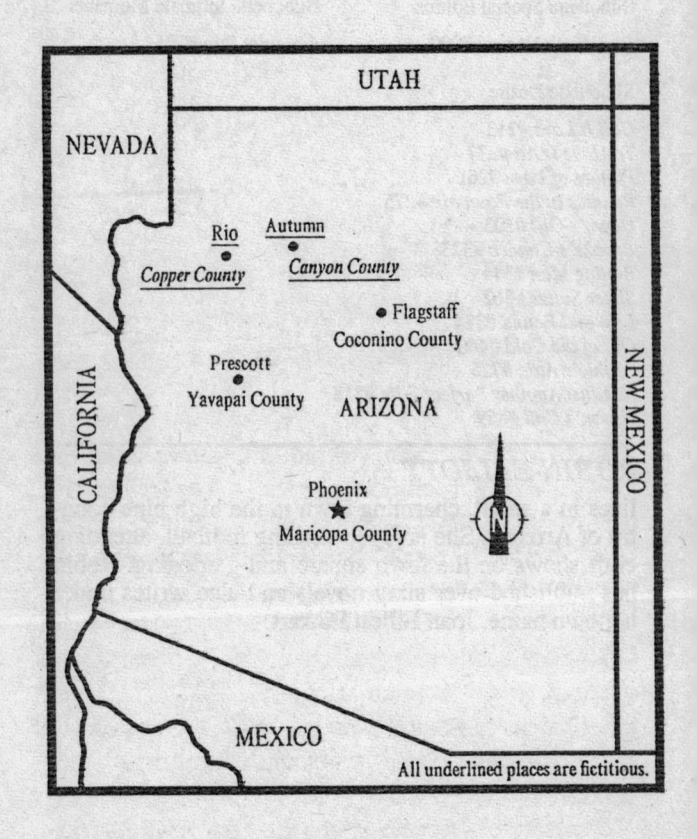

```
                    UTAH
NEVADA
              Rio    Autumn
              •      •
           Copper County  Canyon County

                        • Flagstaff
                        Coconino County

              Prescott
              •
              Yavapai County    ARIZONA

                                        N
                 Phoenix
                 ★
                 Maricopa County

CALIFORNIA                              NEW MEXICO

                    MEXICO
                              All underlined places are fictitious.
```

Chapter One

Large, wet snowflakes drifted lazily down from the ever-darkening clouds in the heavens. The lacy doilies created by Nature's delicate hand began to slowly transform the landscape into a glistening fairyland of pristine white.

Sara Calhoun stood in front of the window in the office, her hands wrapped around her elbows as she stared at the countryside. It was the first snowfall of the year in northern Arizona, and the wondrous beauty it created would be welcomed by most.

But not by Sara.

It was early December; the first snowfall had arrived predictably on time, and with it came haunting memories that caused her to frown and tighten the hold on her arms. Emotions tumbled through her heart and mind in a maze.

Sara shivered, but not from the cold seeping in around the old molding surrounding the window. The chill coursing through her was evoked by the mental scenarios of the past that gave no quarter. She drew a deep, unsteady breath, willing the vivid pictures to fade and return to the dark, dusty corner of her mind where she'd finally been able to place them.

It was so difficult at this moment, she thought. The tall mountain ranges in the distance appearing like ominous sentinels with their snow-topped peaks and the blanket of white that was covering the land combined into a powerful force that was hurling her into a time past where she didn't wish to go.

"Sara Ann."

The sound of the familiar male voice caused her to jerk as she was pulled back to the present. She put a fake smile on her face, then turned to greet the man who had entered the office.

"Hello, Jeb," she said. "The coffee is hot."

Jeb Broffy nodded, then crossed the room to pour himself a mug of the hot brew. Sara watched him go, the smile on her face now genuine.

Dear Jeb, she mused. He had recently celebrated his sixtieth birthday, had a paunch that inched over his belt, was nearly bald but didn't care, and had a heart as big as the entire state of Arizona.

But Jeb Broffy could be tough when the need arose. He had been the sheriff of the city of Autumn, and Canyon County, for more than twenty-five years.

He was an institution in these parts; known by all, respected by the masses, feared by those who dared break the laws Jeb upheld. He was an important part of Sara's life, and she loved him as a daughter would a father.

Jeb took a sip of the steaming coffee and grimaced. "Sludge. Hot sludge. Sara Ann, we've got to do something about the fact that you make the worst coffee in Canyon County."

"No problem. *You* fix it every morning."

Jeb chuckled. "Yours isn't *that* bad. In fact, it's better this way. It makes me appreciate Martha's brew even more."

"Your darling wife is the best cook in Canyon County."

"Now, that's a fact." He moved to behind his desk and sank heavily into the cracked-leather chair, the old piece of furniture creaking in protest.

"You need a new chair."

"There's not a darned thing wrong with this one, Sara Ann."

"Sara. It's Sara, remember? I'm all grown up now, Sheriff, sir. When I moved back here three months ago, I filled in my job application for chief deputy sheriff with the name Sara Calhoun. My identification card as a deputy in good standing of the city of

Autumn and of Canyon County reads Sara Calhoun. Sara, not Sara Ann."

Jeb raised his eyebrows, an expression of innocence on his face. "Are you trying to make a point... Sara Ann?"

Shaking her head and laughing, Sara walked behind her desk and sat on the leather chair, which was slightly newer than Jeb's, but still creaked from her one hundred and fifteen pounds.

"Noisy chair you've got there, girl," Jeb said.

Sara shot him a mock glare, then the two directed their attention to the papers on their desks. The silence in the room was comfortable, born of many years of love.

Fifteen minutes later, Jeb scrawled his name at the bottom of a form he'd completed, then tossed it into a dented wire basket on the corner of his desk.

He switched his gaze to one of the two windows in the office and saw that the falling snow was rapidly changing into a full-blown blizzard, making it impossible to see more than a few feet beyond the window. A whipping wind had come up, whistling its chilly message around the poorly insulated wooden frames of the glass.

Jeb leaned back in his chair and crossed his arms loosely over his chest as he directed his attention to Sara. She was working intently on the report she was preparing, her head bent, allowing Jeb to study her without her knowledge.

Sara Ann Calhoun. Lordy, it was hard to believe she was grown, no longer the child Jeb had known since the day she was born. Having never been blessed with children, he and Martha loved her like a daughter.

She was a pretty one, fairly tall at five foot six, had short, curly black hair, and the same amazing emerald green eyes like her daddy. She looked fine, mighty fine, in the regulation khaki uniform she wore.

He looked at the swirling snow outside, then frowned as he stared at Sara once more.

A blizzard in December, he thought. Sara Ann had to be dealing with some mighty painful memories. What had happened three years ago was as vivid in his mind as though it were yesterday. She was reliving it all, he was certain of it, struggling with the anger and sorrow. But she'd never let on, not give one clue to her distress.

Jeb sighed, shook his head and reached for the next paper on the stack.

Just after six o'clock that night, Sara drove slowly away from the office. She leaned over the steering wheel of her Bronco, straining to see through the thickly falling snow.

Visibility was practically nil, and she hoped the citizens of Autumn were safely home with the intention of staying there. Even the most seasoned winter-weather driver would have difficulty maneuvering in this blizzard.

What normally would be a ten-minute trip took thirty-five white-knuckled minutes, and with a pent-up sigh of relief, Sara finally pressed the button on the garage door opener and drove the vehicle into the welcoming single-car garage.

Twenty minutes later she was showered, had donned a faded floor-length, dark blue velour robe and bright pink socks, and set a match to the waiting kindling in the fireplace.

As the crackling flames leaped higher, engulfing the fragrant mesquite logs she'd set in place that morning, she extended her hands toward the screened hearth to savor the warmth.

Time lost meaning as she became mesmerized by the nearly hypnotic fire.

She'd missed having a fireplace when she'd lived in the small apartment while attending Colorado State University. But her budget hadn't allowed for any luxuries as she'd studied to obtain a degree in law enforcement.

Every spare moment and penny she'd had was devoted toward achieving her ultimate goal, which she'd just accomplished—passing the difficult requirements of the National Search and Rescue Association.

A rumbling in her stomach brought her back to reality with the undeniable message that she was hungry.

She turned from the fireplace with the intention of going into the kitchen to determine what might tempt her in the way of dinner, then stopped, her gaze sweeping over the living room.

She'd grown up in this small two-bedroom house. Her first steps had been taken here, her first words spoken. She'd laughed and cried within these walls, and she had been loved by a father whom she'd loved just as much.

Her mother was a vague, fleeting memory of a woman who had simply walked away from her husband and four-year-old daughter.

Virginia Calhoun had left a brief but damning note scribbled on the back of an envelope. She wanted more from life than the dull existence in Autumn with its population of three thousand easygoing, laid-back people.

Patrick Calhoun's world, which had centered on his wife, daughter and rather hand-to-mouth antique business, did not offer her the excitement she craved. She no longer had the desire nor patience to perform in her capacity of a mother, found the role unfulfilling and tedious.

She was leaving and had no intention of ever coming back.

Sara stared unseeing across the room as her mind flitted back in time. Patrick had left her with Martha and Jeb Broffy for two weeks, then suddenly reappeared. He announced that he'd thought it all through during those days of solitude, and had decided that *he'd* raise Sara Ann himself, they'd be a team and, by damn, they'd do just fine.

And they had.

A soft smile touched Sara's lips as scene after scene tumbled through her mind of events shared with her father.

She saw herself giddy with excitement and ready for the first day of school, clad in a yellow pinafore badly in need of ironing, and wearing one red and one green sock. Her daddy had told her she would be the prettiest girl in Mrs. Fisher's kindergarten class, and Sara Ann had believed him. She'd also punched Joey Swanson square in the nose for making fun of her mismatched socks.

There had been birthday parties with day-old bakery cakes, one with the inscription Happy 50th Birthday, Ralph spelled out in purple frosting.

Christmases had produced spindly, lopsided trees that they'd decorated together, and presents wrapped in the colored funnies from the Sunday papers.

Sara had become the keeper of the house as she grew older, managing to prepare simple meals. She shopped for groceries, a chore her absentminded father gave little thought to.

To rely on Patrick for anything other than a bright smile, bear hugs and endless love would have been a study in frustration. Patrick's head was in the clouds, but his heart belonged to Sara Ann.

She had forgiven Patrick for his shortcomings without question. He was her dad, and she loved him just as he was. But as the years passed, she learned without any doubt that if something of importance needed to be done, it was up to her to see to it. She turned to no one for help, for in her mind's eye there was no one there.

Another rumbly protest from her empty stomach jolted Sara from her memory-filled thoughts. She walked across the room, running her fingertips along the top of her father's favorite chair as she passed by.

That awful decrepit chair, she thought, laughing softly. The tweed fabric was faded, the material on the arms worn through in spots, the cushion was mashed nearly flat from years of use. It was Patrick Calhoun's chair, where he'd sat during the evenings for as long as Sara could remember.

She wouldn't even consider having it repaired and upholstered, nor would she sit in it. That chair would stay where it was, as it was, a reminder of loving, happy times now gone but not forgotten.

Sara was dreaming about snow—cold, swirling, nearly blinding snow. In every direction she turned, she was met by a wall of white, making it impossible to move forward.

She was all alone, the snow up to her knees and quickly rising higher, threatening to bury her where she stood. Her scream for help went unanswered.

She was alone in the bone-chilling cold.

Alone in the snow.

And she was terrified.

A sob caught in her throat as she sat bolt upright in bed, her heart racing, eyes widened in fear.

She blinked several times, then took a wobbly breath. With her arms wrapped around her drawn-up legs, she rested her forehead on her knees, willing her heart to slow to a normal rhythm.

Moments later, the telephone on the nightstand rang, the shrill sound causing her to gasp.

She reached for the receiver, ignoring the trembling in her hand, and cut off the noise of the third ring. The glowing clock on the nightstand announced that it was 4:22 a.m.

"Yes?" she said, the receiver to her ear. "Hello?"

"Sara Ann, it's Jeb. I'm at the office, and I need you to come in."

Sara stiffened, her senses on red alert, her entire focus centered on what Jeb was saying. The nightmare that had awakened her was forgotten, the wild thudding of her heart was now caused by Jeb's words.

"What is it, Jeb? What's wrong?"

"Sara Ann, I'm sorry this happened now because I know that you—"

"Jeb," she interrupted, "what is it?"

He cleared his throat, and when he spoke again his tone was strictly business. "We have a report," he said, "of three overdue hunters who went out before the blizzard hit and haven't come back. I've already called the Department of Emergency Services for a mission number, so I need you to report to me in your capacity as the Incident Commander for the Canyon County Sheriff's Office Search and Rescue Response Team. Move it, Calhoun. Get your butt in here *now*."

Chapter Two

There was an eerie ambience to the predawn as Sara drove slowly and carefully along the snow-covered streets of Autumn.

The snow had stopped falling and the sky had cleared, revealing the moon and a multitude of glittering stars. The luminescence from the heavens caused the deep snow to appear as though it had been generously sprinkled with sparkling diamonds.

The simplistic beauty of Nature's touch was not appreciated in the least by Sara. There was, it seemed, a strange stillness, an unsettling quietness, that heightened her sense of unease and provided no buffer from the tormenting thoughts slamming against her mind.

As she'd dressed and prepared to leave the house to drive to the sheriff's office, she'd fought the urge to flee, to get into her vehicle and leave Autumn as quickly as possible.

Three hunters were overdue and considered lost. It was now up to the Search and Rescue Back Country Unit to step in and find the missing people.

She was the Incident Commander for the mission, the one to make the decisions. Lives were at stake. Errors in judgment regarding the best strategy with which to proceed could mean the difference between life and death.

Death.

"No," she whispered, her hold on the steering wheel tightening. "Dear God, no."

She wasn't ready for this, *not yet*. It had taken all her emotional strength to return to Autumn, to move into the house she'd once shared with her father. She had been going slowly, with careful steps as unsteady as a toddler learning to walk, into the arena that held excruciatingly painful memories.

But now, outside forces were dictating her actions, forcing her into a place far from where she was prepared to go.

She couldn't do this.

Damn it, Sara Calhoun, she admonished herself, *you have no choice.* She had to tough up and shut up, put aside her personal turmoil and perform in the role for which she had been trained.

Her ultimate goal during the past three years had been to return to Autumn with fine-tuned expertise in Search and Rescue. The Law Enforcement degree she'd obtained would make it possible for her to take charge in an official capacity, *not as a hit-and-miss volunteer.*

To her disappointment, none of the four deputies currently on Jeb Broffy's staff felt they were candidates for the intense training she would provide to start to build the Canyon County team.

Their reasons were legitimate: it would take too much time from their families, they did not wish to take on the added stress and pressure, and the financial compensation was not enough to offset the endless hours of training.

That left her, she knew, taking charge of a volunteer unit, a fact she was not ready to deal with. *Not yet.* She had been prepared to start her own team, knowing they would receive the finest training.

But work with volunteers? No. She had not even inquired, since her return to Autumn, as to what volunteer units were now in existence in the near area. She had not wanted to know. *Not yet.*

It was all to have been accomplished according to *her* emotional timetable. The call that had come from Jeb tonight was not to have taken place... not yet.

She couldn't do this.

Not yet!

Sara smacked one glove-covered palm against the steering wheel in self-disgust.

She was acting like a panicked child. The sheriff's office was now within view, and she had about five minutes to get herself together and be ready to take action. She could, and she would. Dear heaven, she had to.

She parked in front of the building housing the sheriff's office. Drawing in a deep breath, she let it out slowly, then got out of the vehicle. A battered and rusted pickup truck she didn't recognize was next to Jeb's patrol car, and beyond that was another patrol car that belonged to the deputy on the night shift.

She reached for the handle to open the door to the building, then hesitated.

"Do it," she told herself aloud.

The squaring of her shoulders and the lifting of her chin gave her a mental push. She yanked open the door and entered the brightly lit building, unaware of the inviting warmth that greeted her.

Before she had time to falter, Jeb appeared in the hallway and jerked his head in the direction of the office they shared. Sara followed him, concentrating on producing a professional this-is-all-in-a-day's-work expression, hoping it didn't look as phony as it felt.

Jeb turned to face her in the middle of the room.

"Are you all right?" he asked quietly, a frown of concern knitting his brows.

"Of course," she said, not meeting his gaze directly. She removed her gloves and jacket, then laid them on her desk. "Fill me in, Jeb. What facts do we have?"

She leaned back against the desk and crossed her arms loosely over her chest, striving for a posture and appearance of alert but calm.

"It's Hux," he said. "Frank Huxley, and his two teenage boys. They set out in that old Jeep of theirs yesterday morning and were due back by nightfall.

"Hux got drawn for hunting elk. The family was counting on him bagging one, as it would be their source of meat for many months because they've been having a real rough time financially. This wasn't a hunting trip for fun, sport and pleasure. Hux and the boys went out knowing they had to bring home meat for their table."

"I see. That's a negative element, Jeb. They're liable to take chances that regular sport hunters wouldn't. Whose pickup is that out front?"

"Mavis Huxley drove in. She's Hux's wife."

"Yes, I know Mavis. I know the whole family. Hux gave me my first horseback ride on that old plow nag of theirs when I was five years old. I was thrilled right down to my mismatched socks. Hux knows those woods and mountains better than most. That's a plus."

Jeb nodded. "True, but that blizzard created whiteout conditions. Even Frank Huxley could lose his way in that. Mavis waited until after the snow stopped, but when they still didn't show, she drove in. They don't have a phone because they can't afford one anymore. The daughter has moved back home after a divorce and brought three little ones. She's out there at the house, but it will be hard to keep in touch with her without a telephone, to know if they came in. That's another problem you'll have to solve somehow."

"Well, I need to talk to Mavis. How is she holding up through this?"

"She's frightened, but hanging in there."

"Fine. There's information I need to gather so I can decide—"

"Sara Ann," Jeb interrupted, "I've put in a call to the Copper County Sheriff, requesting the assistance of their Volunteer Back Country unit. They're on their way."

A chill of such intensity swept through Sara that she had to grip the edge of the desk to keep from swaying on her feet.

"Volunteers," she said, hardly above a whisper. "The glory boys who play macho games with people's lives."

"Sara Ann, don't. That may have been true of the bunch who came in three years ago, but they were disbanded right after what happened here. You don't know this other unit. I do, because I've brought them in before. They're good men. They're out of Rio, and headed up by Gabe Porter."

"Volunteer units are a menace, Jeb. I don't want them here."

"Well, you're sure as hell going to have them. You'd better work on your attitude before they get here. Are you hearing me, miss?"

Sara opened her mouth to retort, then snapped it closed again and nodded.

"Good. I'll take you in to talk to Mavis." He paused. "By the way, Gabe wasn't too happy to learn that the Incident Commander was academy trained with only simulated field experience."

Sara straightened, her eyes blazing with anger. "That man is questioning my ability to lead this mission?"

"All I know," he said, with a shrug, "is that he said a book jockey is a pain in the butt. Yep, that's a direct quote."

"We'll just see about that," she said, starting across the room. "The nerve of that jerk. Gabriel is liable to meet up with his legendary angels sooner than he expected, because I will have strangled him with my bare hands. Book jockey. Oh, that's despicable."

Jeb chuckled softly and followed Sara as she stomped out of the office.

Sara Ann was mad as hell, he mused. That was fine for now. She couldn't dwell on the past if she was spitting fire in the present. The fact remained, though, that even if a man named Gabriel was on the way to Autumn, his teaming up with Sara Ann Calhoun was not going to be a match made in heaven.

Mavis Huxley was in her late-forties, but appeared ten years older. There was a weariness about her, not born just of worry and a lack of sleep, but from years of hard work and barely managing to scrape by.

Sara had greeted Mavis warmly upon entering the room that held a desk and a medium-size rectangular table surrounded by six metal folding chairs. Mavis sat at the table, her hands gripped tightly in her lap.

Hux and their sons, Bobby, aged fifteen, and Mike, seventeen, had set off at dawn to hunt elk, Mavis related to Sara. Hux carried their only rifle; the boys went along to lend a hand in field-dressing the elk, then help pack it out.

"What were they wearing?" Sara asked. She sat opposite Mavis at the table, taking notes as Mavis supplied the information needed.

Dale Maddox, the deputy on the night shift, and Jeb sat at the opposite end of the table.

"They were bundled up good," Mavis said. "I saw to that. They have on long johns, flannel shirts, pullover sweaters and their puffy padded jackets. They're wearing jeans and lace-up work boots with two pairs of socks each. I fussed at them to put on the wool caps I knitted and they did, but there's no telling if they took them off the minute they were out of my sight."

She hoped they'd kept the caps on, Sara thought, jotting notes on the pad. Up to fifty percent of a person's body heat could be retained if they wore a hat, preferably one made of wool.

"I assume they had gloves," Sara said.

"Oh, yes, I knit wool mittens for us all."

Mavis continued to answer Sara's questions. Hux was fifty-five now and fit as a fiddle, bless his heart. The Huxleys had just had a hard year is all, as folks weren't hiring a handyman as often with money so tight. Then their girl had moved home with her babies, and they were all pulling together as a family to make ends meet.

Their jackets? Oh, they were sort of a mud-brown color, all three of them. They weren't fancy, just sturdy, warm brown coats, the same color as the caps and mittens.

Sara inwardly groaned, having hoped to hear that the jackets and caps were vivid colors, which would be much easier to spot in the snow-covered area.

"I'm glad to know Hux is in good shape," Sara said. "How about the boys?"

"My stars, yes," Mavis said, the first hint of a smile appearing on her pale face. "We Huxleys are from sound stock, Sara Ann. Now then, you're a tad skinny, but your daddy was a bean pole, so there's just no help for it, I guess."

Dale Maddox laughed. Jeb chuckled. Both received a glare from Sara.

"Does Hux still smoke?" Sara asked.

"Rolls his own. He uses Bull Durham like he always has."

"What provisions did they have, Mavis? You know, food, water, that sort of thing."

"I packed a lunch. Let's see now. I made two big sandwiches each, put in apples, raisins and a whole batch of brownies. We only have one thermos so I filled it with steaming coffee. I figured the boys were old enough to drink coffee now. Other years I sent along hot chocolate. Bobby has one of those backpack things, so I put the food in there. That pack is brown, just like the jackets. The boys are as tall as Hux now, Sara Ann, standing six feet like their daddy. They're good, strong, strapping boys."

Sara smiled. "And handsome as the day is long, I imagine, like their daddy."

"Oh, my, yes," Mavis said, looking extremely pleased. "They are that."

"Mavis," Sara said, leaning slightly toward her, "this is very important, so take your time answering. Did Hux say anything, anything at all, about where he planned to start hunting on foot? He would have driven the Jeep in as far as possible, then set off. It would be extremely helpful if we knew what his plans were."

"No need to ponder it," Mavis said. "Hux has had the same route for years. He's been mighty lucky with bagging his game, so he's a tad superstitious about staying in the same area."

"That's wonderful," Sara said, smiling again. "Okay, I'm going to write it all down, so give it to me slowly, every detail."

"Well, they drive into the woods as far as they can at the base of Thinker's Thumb. You know, that peak of the mountains that looks like a big old thumb. Then they start straight up. I suppose they'd go left or right if they saw tracks of game, but that's where they begin... at the bottom of Thinker's Thumb."

"Fair enough," a deep male voice said. "Knowing that, we'll just go in, find them, and have them home in time for a good hot dinner."

Sara's head snapped up at the sound of the man's voice, and her eyes collided with those of the tall figure standing in the doorway.

Gabriel Porter, no doubt, Sara thought, with a flash of anger. The glory boys had arrived, and their unit leader, the cocky creep, was already making promises to Mavis that he had no way of knowing he could keep.

Oh, he looked the part of a hero to the rescue. Sara would give him that much. He was tall, six-two or three, had wide shoulders and long legs. He was fairly good-looking... well, okay, more than that. He was drop-dead gorgeous, which he was probably very aware of.

His hair was as black as her own, his being thick, a bit tousled at the moment, and in need of a trim. His eyes were very dark, framed in spiky dark lashes. He had a tan, even in the middle of winter, and craggy, rough-hewn features that made Sara think he was about to launch into a commercial spiel for cigarettes or after-shave. His lips were nice, very nice, masculine and definitely kissable.

"Sara Ann," Jeb said, jolting her back to attention as he got to his feet, "close your mouth. Howdy, Gabe, it's good to see you."

Sara snapped her mouth closed and bent her head in an attempt to give the impression that she was reviewing her notes. She could feel the heated flush of embarrassment on her cheeks.

How mortifying, she thought. She hadn't realized her mouth had dropped open as she'd stared at Gabriel Porter. Stared? Lord, she'd been gawking like an adolescent. And that darn Jeb Broffy just had to bring that fact to the attention of everyone in the room. Men were duds, the whole motley lot of them.

As Gabe crossed the room to shake Jeb's and Dale's offered hands, Sara slid a glance in his direction from beneath her lashes.

The funny flutter in the pit of her stomach was hereby declared to be totally ignored, she decided. So what if his black jeans and black sweater outlined that magnificent physique to perfection? So what if he moved with controlled, athletic grace, a smooth, criminally sensual gait? So what if he could win the Best-Buns-of-the-Year-Award?

"Sara Ann?" Jeb said.

"What?" she said, a grumpy tone to her voice. She stared unseeing at the pad of paper in front of her. "Oh," she said in the next instant. She got to her feet and turned toward Jeb, a rather bland, bored expression on her face. "Yes, Jeb?"

"I'd like you to meet Gabriel Porter, the head honcho of the Copper County Back Country Unit," Jeb said. "Gabe, this young lady is your official Incident Commander, Sara Ann Calhoun."

"Sara," she said, automatically correcting Jeb's use of Sara Ann. She'd have Gabriel Porter call her Miss

Calhoun. Yes, good idea. She was in charge, and she'd firmly establish that fact right now. "Mr. Porter," she said coolly, with a slight dip of her head.

Gabe looked at her for a long, silent moment before starting slowly toward her, his eyes never leaving hers. As he came down the length of the table, the tempo of Sara's heart increased with every blatantly masculine step he took. He turned at the end of the table and stopped in front of her. "Sara," he said, still looking directly into her eyes. "That's a pretty name, has a lovely ring of old-fashionedness to it. You call me Gabe, since you've invited me to call you Sara."

She certainly had not, Sara thought. She'd been replacing Jeb's use of Sara Ann with Sara, that's all. Gabriel Porter was to refer to her as Miss Calhoun, and she was about to deliver that message.

"Sara will be fine," she heard herself say. Where had that come from? her mind yelled. "Yes, well," she said, clearing her throat. She switched her gaze to Mavis. "This is Mavis Huxley. We're going into the field to find her husband and two teenage sons."

"Mrs. Huxley," Gabe said, nodding at Mavis. "Try not to worry. We'll bring your menfolk home to you."

Sudden tears filled Mavis's eyes, and she pressed trembling fingertips to her lips for a moment, striving to control her emotions.

"Thank you," she said, her voice quivering. "Sara Ann has asked me so many questions, very businesslike, and I've done my best to answer them as best I could. Don't misunderstand, Sara Ann. I'm not faulting you for doing your job in the proper manner. It's just that I needed to hear someone say that Hux and the boys will be all right, even though I know it's not a God-given promise. That sounds very foolish, I guess, but I do thank you for the kind words, Mr. Porter."

A painful knot tightened in Sara's stomach as she listened to Mavis's tear-filled voice, the words beating against Sara's mind.

She'd been too clinical, too detached, she admonished herself. But how else was she to be able to gather the vitally important information she needed? False hope and worthless promises simply had no place in fact-finding dialogue.

Then in walks arrogant Gabriel Porter, who immediately assures Mavis Huxley that everything will be fine and dandy. Mavis proceeds to thank the man for saying so, at the same time she's acknowledging that she realizes it might not be true.

Damn, this just didn't make sense, Sara thought. Well, she couldn't dwell on it now. Time was the enemy. They had to get out into the field and find the Huxleys.

"Mavis," Jeb said, moving to her side, "you come into my office with me. I'll phone Martha and have her drive over and take you to our place. There's a radio at the house that I can call in on and give you news as we get it. There's no sense your being here. You'll be much better off with Martha."

When Mavis, Jeb and Dale had left the room, Sara looked at Gabe, lifting her chin as she met his gaze.

"Please summon your men into this room, Mr. Porter. I need to brief them on the information I've gotten from Mavis Huxley, and tell them how I wish to proceed with the mission."

"Yes, ma'am," he said, grinning as he saluted her. "Anything you say, ma'am. You're the boss of this outfit." He turned and strode from the room.

You've got that straight, buster, Sara thought, with a decisive nod. The first order she ought to issue should be that Gabriel Porter was not allowed to smile that knock-'em-dead smile. Lord, the man even had a dimple in his right cheek. Not fair, not fair at all.

Forget it, Sara, she told herself in the next instant. The important thing was the mission at hand. They would find Hux, Bobby and Mike, and bring them home, alive and well. Everything would be fine.

It just had to be.

Chapter Three

Sara Calhoun, Gabe mused, as he started down the hallway. Sara Ann. He really hadn't formed a mental picture of the woman Jeb Broffy had said would be the Incident Commander of the search.

The minute the telephone call had come, he'd shifted to mental and physical alertness, clicking off in his mind who to contact and what needed to be done to reach Autumn as quickly as possible. His feelings regarding having a book jockey in charge were made clear to Jeb, who had, quite frankly, ignored Gabe's grumbling.

When he'd walked into that room and seen Sara, he'd felt as though he'd been punched in the gut. She was sensational, did enticingly female things for a deputy's khaki uniform that had caused an instantaneous coil of heat to tighten low in his body.

She was slender but definitely, *most definitely,* had delectable feminine curves in all the right places. Her dark curls appeared silky, would slide through a man's fingers like satin threads, and her features were delicate. Sara wasn't beautiful, she was... yes, lovely—fresh, wholesome, pretty as a picture.

And Lord, those eyes. Those emerald green eyes of hers were capable of turning a man inside out. Miss Sara Ann Calhoun was really something.

"Hey, Gabe," one of the men said as he approached, "what have we got?"

An Incident Commander like none we've ever seen before, Chuck, Gabe thought, as he stopped in front of the group.

"Let's go," he said, jerking his head in the direction of the room he'd just come from. "The quicker we get the briefing taken care of, the sooner we can hit the road. Chuck, did you make the calls?"

"Yep, sure did."

Gabe nodded, and the men started quickly back down the hallway.

"Do we really have a woman Incident Commander?" one of the men said.

"Yep," Gabe said. "There's no doubt at all that she's a woman, Ben."

"Well, hell," Ben said, "that ought to slow things down to a snail's crawl. A woman can't set a pace to match a man's, Gabe."

"You never know," he said. "Women are amazing creatures."

"Well, yeah, you've got that straight," Ben said, chuckling. "They can drive a guy right out of his ever-lovin' mind quicker than anything I know."

The other men laughed, but the moment they entered the room for the briefing, they sobered and were strictly business.

These men, Gabe knew, glancing over at them, were some of the best Search and Rescue people in the state. He'd trained them, knew how dedicated they were, how skilled, how determined to succeed. He'd trusted them with his life on more than one occasion, and would do so again with no hesitation.

"Sara," Gabe said, "these are the members of your team. This is Chuck, Ben, Billy and Moses. Gentlemen, meet Sara Calhoun, our Incident Commander."

Sara stepped forward and extended her hand, shaking each man's in turn, as she looked directly into his eyes.

Chuck and Ben, she mentally cataloged, appeared, like Gabe, to be in their mid-thirties. Billy was younger, was maybe twenty-three or twenty-four. Those three were nicely built, with muscles and no extra fat.

But Moses? Good grief, he had to be at least fifty, if not older. While that certainly wouldn't be considered old in the everyday mainstream of life, in the strenuous world encompassed by a Search and Rescue Unit, it was ancient.

Not only that, Moses didn't have the bulk and muscle the other men did. He was only a couple of inches taller than Sara and had a wiry build. Well, so be it. They'd find out soon enough that she wasn't slowing her pace so Moses could keep up.

"Please be seated," Sara said, sweeping one arm in the direction of the table.

"Chuck," Gabe said, as they settled into their chairs, "fill Sara in on the information you gathered with the telephone calls."

"There are no helicopters available at the moment," Chuck said. "If they're freed up later in the day, it won't do us any good as there's another heavy snowstorm due to hit in a few hours. We've got about ten inches of snow on the ground now in higher elevations. Autumn is at seventy-five hundred feet. Where are we headed?"

"Thinker's Thumb," Sara said.

Chuck nodded. "The Thumb is eight thousand feet at the base, and ten thousand feet at the top. Plenty of snow. Guaranteed. The horse posse can't get in even now, so don't count on them. The Jeep posse over in Yavapai County is on standby, but we might as well cancel them if we're doing the Thumb. That's it, that's all I've got."

Sara remained standing at the head of the table. "Thank you."

All of the men were looking at her, which was as it should be. The details Sara was about to give them during this briefing were extremely important.

But while she had their undivided attention, she could *feel* Gabriel Porter's gaze, actually feel it, along with the heat his penetrating dark eyes were causing to swirl within her.

Darn it, it was bad enough that she had to work with volunteers. The fact that the unit leader was having an unsettling sensual impact on her was intolerable. Well, as of right now, she was putting an end to *that* adolescent nonsense.

She wouldn't be interested in Gabe Porter as a man under any circumstances, the cocky so-and-so, and there certainly wasn't a place for feminine reactions to a blatantly sexual, masculinity-personified man during a Search and Rescue mission.

"All right," she said, lifting her chin. "I'll fill you in on what I've learned from Mavis Huxley. We're searching for three males. Hux is..."

Sara consulted her notes often as she relayed what Mavis had told her. She then asked the men to join her at the far wall where a large map was hung. The group followed her across the room.

"Excuse me, ma'am," Moses said. "You said Frank Huxley rolls his own cigarettes. Did you happen to ask what kind of tobacco he uses?"

"Oh," Sara said, scrutinizing her notes again. She looked at Moses. "Bull Durham. Why?"

"Dunno," Moses said, shrugging. "Might be useful, might not."

Dandy, Sara thought dryly, turning to the map. Not only was Moses nearly as ancient as his name implied, but he was a good ole boy, who was wasting precious time by asking foolish questions.

"We'll drive as far as we possibly can up Thinker's Thumb," Sara said, pointing to the map. "Wherever the terrain stops us will be our base camp.

"Jeb will stay by the radio here, one of his deputies will take a portable set to the Huxleys' house. I'll have Jeb send a deputy to the Thumb to be in place at the base camp to receive our transmissions. He can start out from here about a half an hour after we do.

"What radio equipment do you have?" she asked Gabe, looking somewhere above his right shoulder.

"Our vehicles have standard two-way radios. We all have hand-helds for the search."

"Fine. I have a hand-held walkie-talkie, too. I'll tune to your frequency. We'll start with a Line Search with two hundred yards between each of us."

Gabe frowned. "You can miss an army squadron by spreading out that far."

"I'm aware of that, Mr. Porter," she said stiffly. "I was about to add that I want a Hasty-Line Search, using a Zigzag pattern."

"Much better," he said, smiling at her.

Sara glared at him, then swept her gaze over the men. "Any questions?" No one spoke. "Fine. Let's get on it, gentlemen. With road conditions what they are, it will take us about an hour to get to the Thumb. Time, per usual, is one of our enemies."

"Saddle up, cowpokes," Moses said, grinning.

Oh, good Lord, Sara thought, marching from the room. She didn't need this. Saddle up, cowpokes? Gabriel Porter had to be out of his tiny mind to have included Moses in this unit. Heaven save her from volunteers.

As the group came down the hallway, Martha Broffy entered the building through the front door. She was short and plump, and appeared even rounder due to the heavy coat she wore. A knitted scarf covered her head, revealing just a glimpse of curly gray hair. A smile lit up her face when she saw Sara.

"Hello, dear," Martha said.

Sara quickened her step to reach Martha, then hugged her.

"Good morning, Martha," she said. "Well, it's morning, but I'm not sure how good it is."

"Yes, I know. Poor Mavis. This has got to be so difficult for her." Martha studied Sara's face. "This crisis must be difficult for you, as well, Sara Ann. How are you doing, dear?"

Sara stiffened slightly, acutely aware that Gabe and his men had stopped just a few feet behind her and could hear what Martha was saying.

"Heavenly days, Martha," Sara said, a bit too loudly, "I'm fine. We're ready to head out, everything is under control, and my only complaint is that

I was forced to leave my toasty-warm bed earlier than usual."

"I see," Martha said quietly, no hint of a smile now on her face. She looked past Sara. "Hello, Gabriel. You haven't been over our way in a while."

Gabe smiled. "You're looking as beautiful as ever, Martha. You know all of these rotten guys."

"Indeed I do. Chuck, Ben, Billy, Moses... hello to you all. I best put on a huge pot of stew. I've fed the bunch of you after a search, and you surely can pack it away. I'll have a hot meal waiting for you."

"Can't ask for better than that," Gabe said.

"Let's go get the Huxleys," Billy said. "I want my share of Martha's stew."

"Consider it done," Gabe said.

"Nothing is going to get done," Sara said, "if we stand here talking about it."

"You're absolutely right, ma'am," Gabe said, grinning. "Grab your jackets, boys. Do you have snow chains on your tires, Sara?"

"Not yet."

"No sense wasting time doing it now," he said. "You and I can go in my vehicle, the others in Chuck's. That will leave room in mine to bring the Huxleys out if need be. Their Jeep may be half-buried in snow by now. They can always go back after it later."

"Yes, well..." Sara started.

"Ready?" Gabe said.

Sara glared at him again, went into Jeb's office, requested that a deputy be sent to the base camp, another to the Huxleys' house, and returned wearing her jacket. She kissed Martha on the cheek, and the six left the building.

After Sara transferred her gear to Gabe's vehicle, they started out, Chuck following close behind.

There was now enough early light for Sara to be able to study a map of the terrain of Thinker's Thumb, and the first fifteen minutes of the drive was made in silence. She finally refolded the map and placed it next to her on the seat.

She glanced at Gabe, reluctantly admitting that he commanded the vehicle with ease and expertise. Even with snow chains, driving was difficult with the present condition of the roads. Gabe was as relaxed as someone on a Sunday outing.

Gabe and his men, Sara noted, were wearing fleece jackets like her own, which had surprised her. The expedition jackets were state-of-the-art, complete with "pit zips" beneath the arms to vent body heat. Even in the coldest weather, mountain climbing was sweaty work, and it was imperative that the hiker keep his clothes dry and his body temperature normal.

Fine, they all had the proper jackets, but there was much more to being equipped to be able to perform to the maximum of one's abilities. Every spare penny she'd earned had gone toward the top-of-the-line gear that she'd carefully investigated.

At the base camp, she would be putting on the finest cold weather outerwear on the market. It was lightweight, wind and waterproof, yet allowed the body to breathe naturally.

She'd add gauntlet gloves that would cover her hands and snap into place above the wrist, and gaiters over her leather boots. The gaiters were styled after spats, zipped up to below the knees, then tightened with drawstrings.

Those extra pieces of equipment made a tremendous difference in warmth, and the ability to keep snow from creeping into boots and up sleeves.

More than one victim's life had been saved by the fact that the rescue unit wore high-quality gear, making it possible to stay out in the elements hours longer than a unit with inferior equipment.

Oh, Sara, shut up, she admonished herself. She was conducting a mental equipment inventory to avoid squaring off against the knot in her stomach and the whisper of haunting ghosts in her mind.

She had to focus on *this* search, not the one that had been botched three years ago.

The mission was to find Frank, Bobby and Mike Huxley, not dwell on the fact that her father had died of hypothermia because the team looking for him had misread a sign that was as clear as day.

She was the Incident Commander this time. Her team was made up of volunteers, unfortunately, but *she* was fully and expertly trained, and these men were going to follow *her* orders.

If any one of them gave the slightest indication that he didn't intend to do this her way, she would ship him back to base camp.

And that went for the arrogant Mr. Gabriel Porter, as well.

Chapter Four

Gabe glanced over at Sara to see that she was looking out of the side window. He quickly redirected his attention to the snow-covered road, then automatically checked the rearview mirror to be certain that Chuck wasn't having problems maneuvering his vehicle in the snow.

Martha Broffy's words echoed in Gabe's mind.

This crisis must be difficult for you, as well, Sara Ann.

Gabe frowned. What had Martha meant? he wondered. Maybe it was nothing more than the fact that Sara was taking part in her first real Search and Rescue mission. Jeb had mentioned that tidbit when he'd telephoned, which had not thrilled Gabe one iota.

Since there was obviously a close relationship between Sara and the Broffys, Martha could have been simply clucking over her baby chick like a loving mother hen.

But for some unknown reason, he had a feeling it was more complicated than that. Well, it was none of his business. All he had to worry about was that Sara did an adequate job as Incident Commander of the mission, did not place any of his team in harm's way with glaring errors of judgment.

So far, she was doing fine, albeit being very tense and going strictly by the damn book. As for what Martha had said, he would just forget it.

Ah, hell, no, he wouldn't, he admitted. Sara Ann Calhoun had gotten to him. She'd thrown him off kilter in the man and woman arena, and inched into his emotional sphere.

She was physically desirable, and he couldn't remember when, if ever, he'd been so sexually aware and aroused the instant he'd seen a woman.

Emotionally? She intrigued him, fascinated him, made him want to discover what was beneath the outer facade of I'm-in-charge-here-you-lamebrains. There was something, an unknown something, evident in those incredible emerald eyes of hers. Fear? Pain? He didn't know.

But he intended to find out.

Why? Hell, he didn't know the answer to that question, either.

Well, one thing was for sure. If Sara didn't lighten up a little, she'd be exhausted from the stiff-as-a-board, tense, totally wired control she was exhibiting.

There was nothing casual about the mission, about searching for, and hopefully finding, the three Huxleys alive and well. But there had to be a balance between concentrating on the objective and staying loose enough to be able to draw upon every ounce of physical and mental energy one possessed.

That imperative knowledge a person couldn't learn from a book, nor from simulated field maneuvers. It came with time and experience carrying out actual missions; experience that Sara didn't have.

So, talk to her, Porter, he told himself. He had from here to Thinker's Thumb to attempt to get Sara to unwind a little before she flew straight up in the air like a tightly coiled spring.

"Sara..." he said.

She jerked in her seat and snapped her head around to look at him. "What!"

Very, *very* tense, Gabe thought.

"Jeb mentioned that you grew up in Autumn," he said, producing a pleasant, laid-back tone of voice. "And came back a few months ago after living in Colorado."

"Yes."

"I imagine it's good to be home."

"Yes."

"Autumn is a nice little town."

"Yes."

"Do you still have family there?"

"No."

Gabe sighed and shook his head. "This conversation is so stimulating, I hardly know where to put myself." He paused. "Look, Sara, I realize that as Incident Commander of this mission you have a tremendous responsibility, but we're all in this together. We're a team. You, me, the other members of the unit. All we can do is the best we can do, and we will. You really need to relax."

"Relax?" she said, nearly yelling. "Pretend we're going on a Sunday picnic? That attitude could cost the Huxleys their lives, mister."

A flash of anger swept through Gabe, and he forced himself to slowly count to ten before he spoke again.

"I didn't say what I just did," he said, a muscle ticking in his jaw, "because I like the sound of my own voice. Tension drains a person's physical and mental energies. There's a fine line between being alert, razor sharp, and being so wired that you defeat yourself. That's the point I'm trying to get across here."

"Oh," Sara said quietly. "I... yes, you're right. I was taught all of that at the Department of Public Safety Academy."

"Yeah, well, it's easy for them to stand in front of a class and preach it to students. It's quite another thing for you to put it into practice when you're dealing with the real goods. Keep it in mind. Okay?"

"Yes. Yes, I will." Sara paused. "Thank you."

He smiled at her, then looked at the road again. "You're welcome, ma'am."

Oh, darn, Sara inwardly moaned, there was that smile again, that lethal, toe-curling smile. And that dimple. It was too much, it really was.

How was it possible that in the midst of a critical mission of Search and Rescue, a portion of the very essence of herself was responding to Gabriel Porter on a sensual, purely feminine plane? It certainly didn't bolster her confidence in her role of Incident Commander.

Then to unsettle her even more, Gabe had to bring to her attention the level of tension she was operating under, and the price she might pay because of it.

She *knew* about the danger of being overstressed, had been taught that during her training. She needed to get in touch with herself and regain her inner control.

Damn Gabriel Porter. She didn't know if he annoyed her more when he was cocky, or when he was being sensitive and kind. Any way she looked at it, Gabe got on her nerves.

And if he flashed that devastating smile again, she was definitely going to punch him right in the nose.

"So, Gabe," he said, bringing Sara from her mental fuming, "have you lived in Rio long?" He paused. "Well, let's see. It will be three years in the spring." He paused again. "What do you do there? It is, after all, a small town, hardly bigger than Autumn."

Sara laughed in spite of herself.

"I have a small ranch I inherited from my grandfather," Gabe rambled on. "I call it 'Heaven's Gate,' a befitting moniker for a place that is just this side of heaven and belongs to a guy named Gabriel. In fact, our search unit uses 'Heaven's Gate' as the radio code for 'All is well, the mission has been accomplished.'

"Anyway, I'm a rancher. I run some cattle, a few horses, and grow Christmas trees. I'm a dropout from the fast lane of corporate law in Los Angeles. I got the ranch at about the same time as my second L.A.-induced ulcer, came to Rio, and never looked back."

"Okay, okay," Sara said, smiling. "I get the message. We're not going to arrive at Thinker's Thumb any faster if I sit here and stew about the mission. So, we'll chat, relax, shoot the breeze."

"Bingo."

"All right, where are we? Oh, yes. Do you have a family?"

Family? she mentally repeated. As in wife, children? It hadn't occurred to her that Gabe might be married. That certainly was evidence that her brain wasn't hitting on all cylinders. Good grief, had she been having sexual reactions to a married man?

"I have a regulation set of parents," he said. "One mother, one father. They've retired to Florida. My sister lives in Ohio, and has four kids. Her husband is a dentist. If you want to have your teeth checked, I can get you a good deal, if you're willing to go to Cleveland. Oh, yes, and there's Angel. My beautiful, brown-eyed Angel."

Oh, Sara thought. Well...oh...well, yes, of course, his wife. It stood to reason that a handsome, virile man like Gabriel Porter would be married. That was *not* disappointment she was registering, it was... was...damn, it was disappointment. And *that* was ridiculous. She didn't even like this man.

"Angel is gorgeous," Gabe said, a rather wistful tone to his voice. "She welcomes me home no matter what time I drag myself in. She loves me unconditionally, just as I am. If I show up with people to share dinner, that's fine. If I'm so exhausted I flop on the bed and sleep wearing muddy clothes, no problem. She's really something, my Angel."

"She sounds eligible for sainthood," Sara said under her breath.

Gabe heard her and chuckled. "I wouldn't go that far. She does make certain demands. I might be sound asleep and...blam...she's all over me, wanting me to—"

"Gabe," she interrupted, "I really don't think it's in very good taste to discuss...well, the more intimate side of your relationship with your wife."

"Wife?" he said, raising his eyebrows. "I have an ex-wife, who lives in Los Angeles, but..."

"Then who in the blue blazes is Angel?" Sara said, none too quietly.

"My German shepherd," he said, then hooted with laughter. "Gabriel's Angel. Get it?"

Sara's eyes widened, and in the next instant she slugged him on the arm, immediately realizing it was as solid as a tree trunk.

"Abuse!" Gabe yelled, then fell apart laughing, causing the vehicle to skid for a second on the slick road.

The rich resonance of Gabe's laughter was infectious, and Sara laughed along with him, the air ringing with the joyous sound.

Gabe finally quieted and glanced over at Sara. Their eyes met only for a moment as his attention needed to be directed on the road.

Sara's breath caught, and her smile faded.

There had been something powerful, intense and undefinable, she realized, in that split second when their eyes had held. Heat had suffused her, and a sudden amalgam of confusing emotions had tumbled through her mind.

Dear heaven, Gabe was dangerous. It was the only word she could think of that fully described him. He unsettled her, threw her off balance at every turn, and she didn't like it, not one little bit. She had no intention of falling prey to Gabriel Porter's masculine magnetism. Not Gabe's, nor any other man's, for that matter. Not ever.

Gabe leaned forward over the steering wheel. "There's Thinker's Thumb. Man, look at the snow on that mountain. Check out the horizon, too, Sara. Those clouds are snow-packed, no doubt about it, and they're rolling in fast. Ms. Incident Commander, I'd say we've got our work cut out for ourselves. Big time."

And none too soon, he thought. Desire had rocketed through him with a white-hot flame in that minuscule moment when he'd looked into Sara's eyes. There'd been something else present, too, that he couldn't yet put a name to.

Interesting. This was not the time or place to pursue it, but he sure as hell wasn't going to forget it. Oh, yes, he had unfinished, rather puzzling, business to follow through on with Miss Sara Ann Calhoun.

At the base of the mountain, Gabe drove even slower as he followed a makeshift narrow road produced over the years by vehicles driven as far up the center of the Thumb as was possible. Tall, snow-covered pine trees edged the path. The Forest Service maintained the roads that circled the base of the entire mountain range.

After they had gone about a mile up a steep grade with Chuck following close behind, Sara pointed out the front windshield.

"There," she said. "It's a Jeep. Hux did exactly as Mavis said he would."

"Yep," Gabe said. "That's testimony to the fact that a husband and wife should communicate with each other, just like the experts harp about."

Gabe pulled up on the right-hand side of Frank Huxley's truck. Chuck parked on the left, sandwiching the Jeep between the vehicles.

When everyone got out, Ben immediately went to the Jeep, tried the doors, which proved to be locked, then swept the snow from the front windshield. Moments later he joined the others. The group produced great puffs of white as they breathed the cold air.

"No note," Ben said. "That's typical. He didn't figure on getting stuck up here, so he didn't say which way he was headed in case someone had to come after him."

"Mavis said he'd go straight up," Sara said. "If he saw sign of elk, he'd veer off the trail."

"I hope ole Hux got himself an elk," Billy said. "Ever had elk steak? Now, that is one fine meal."

"All you ever think about is food," Chuck said, smiling.

"And women," Billy said. "Food and women."

"Sounds good to me," Ben said.

"All right, gentlemen," Sara said, no hint of a smile on her face. "Gather your gear, and let's get this mission underway. I'll take the far right edge of the area we'll cover."

"I'm far left," Chuck said.

"Fine," she said. "I have one-inch-wide plastic surveyor's tape with me. That's used for—"

"What color is yours?" Gabe interrupted. "Ours is bright blue."

"Oh," she said. "You know about... Well, good, that's good. Mine is lime green. We'll use that. Chuck, you and I will tie strips to tree branches approximately every fifty feet to mark both of the edging boundaries."

"Roger," Chuck said. "Gabe, what's the altitude at this spot?"

To Sara's astonishment, Gabe swept back the cuff of his jacket and pressed a button on his watch.

"Right around eighty-five hundred feet," he said, looking at the face of the watch. "You said the bottom of the Thumb is at eight thousand so..." He looked up. "The top is ten thousand feet. That ledge we saw as we were coming in is at about nine thousand feet."

Gabe had an altimeter on his watch. That piece of equipment was still on Sara's wish list.

"That ledge," she said, "is where we'll meet. Doing a Zigzag pattern, considering the depth of the snow, and the steep terrain, it should take approximately an hour to get to the ledge. We'll rendezvous there."

"Speaking of snow," Moses said, looking at the sky.

"Yes?" Sara said.

"We're going to get ourselves a bushel of it," Moses said, meeting her gaze. "It's coming in from the northeast, which, in these mountains, means it's going to be a doozy of a storm."

"I realize that, Moses," she said rather stiffly.

He shrugged. "Just thought I'd mention it."

"Gentlemen?" Sara said. "Your gear."

Sara's outerwear was bright turquoise with black trim. She quickly had it snapped, zipped and tied into place, then came around the end of Gabe's vehicle.

What she saw caused her eyes to widen in surprise. All of the men wore outerwear every bit as top of the line as hers. To add to her flustered state, Gabe's was the reverse colors of hers, black with turquoise trim.

Billy had dark blue trimmed in white. Ben had picked yellow with orange, Chuck's was black with white and Moses's iridescent fuchsia. They all had excellent equipment.

The men helped each other put on their backpacks, and Sara slipped hers on, settling the thirty-five-pound load as comfortably as possible into place. The others were carrying sixty to sixty-five pounds each, she surmised, judging from the three-feet-high packs they wore.

Sara gave Chuck a roll of the marking tape, then took a deep breath.

This was it, she thought, a shiver of trepidation coursing through her. She'd worked hard and long for this moment, and now it was here.

Nothing could ever bring her father back, nor totally erase the pain of knowing that he had died due to others' negligence.

But this time, on this rescue mission, Frank Huxley and his sons were going to be found. There would be no needless deaths. She would gather her courage, her physical and emotional energies, and every bit of knowledge she possessed, and bring this search to a successful and proper end.

Sara lifted her chin and squared her shoulders. At that moment, her gaze met Gabe's and his dark eyes pinned her in place.

"Our objective," he said quietly, "is Heaven's Gate."

"Amen," Moses said.

Chapter Five

It was bitter cold, and the going was slow, due to the depth of the snow and the fact that they were continually climbing. The Zigzag pattern Sara had instructed them to implement required them to move back and forth, as well as ascending.

Sara blanked her mind of everything but the climb, concentrating on her footing, and watching carefully for any sign, any evidence at all, that the Huxleys had traveled that same terrain.

She could feel the pull of her leg muscles, now grateful for the grueling hours she'd spent in a physical conditioning program. Her breathing was steady, puffs of white visible each time she exhaled.

From her position on the far right edge of the group, she could see only Gabe and Ben, the others out of view around the curve of Thinker's Thumb.

Gabe was higher than she was but, she reasoned, he wasn't stopping to tag bushes and trees with the lime-colored tape. She could keep up with Gabriel Porter, no doubt about it.

Her trepidation had vanished as they'd officially begun the search. This was what she'd trained so hard and long for. She knew what to do, and how to do it.

And having a unit made up of volunteers added to the challenge. She was in her element, where she belonged, and it was invigorating.

They were going to find the Huxleys and bring them safely home!

As Sara went higher, the mountain narrowed, causing her to lose sight of Gabe. The nightmare she'd had suddenly flickered in her mind's eye as she realized she was alone, surrounded by snow. She forced the memory of the dream away and pushed on, heading for the ledge above, where she would rendezvous with the others.

It took Sara closer to an hour and a half, rather than the hour she'd estimated, to reach the ledge. She was, she admitted, very ready for a short rest. It would be interesting to see at what intervals the others showed up at the ledge, especially Moses.

Finally at the ledge, she worked her way around toward the center, still watching for sign of the Huxleys. When she covered the last curve, she stopped dead in her tracks, her eyes widening.

Moses was hunkered down behind a small camp stove, lazily stirring something in a pot set on the flames. The others were removing their packs, obviously having arrived moments before her. She shrugged out of her backpack and quickened her step, her gaze sweeping over the group when she halted in front of the little stove.

"Moses?" she said, staring at him. "How did you... how long have you been up here?"

"A bit of time," he said, continuing to look into the pot.

Gabe chuckled. "Long enough to make hot chocolate, which is going to be great going down all the way to cold toes. Serve it up, Moses. We're ready."

"Yep." Moses reached for one of the metal mugs stacked by the stove.

"Moses," Sara said quietly, "I don't know what to say. I owe you an apology because I was certain you wouldn't be able to keep the pace. I'm sorry."

Moses handed her a mug. "No need to be. It's a mistake a lot of folks make. Age doesn't mean squat in Search and Rescue. That's a fact."

"Indeed it is." She took a sip of the hot drink. "Oh, this is wonderful."

Gabe accepted his mug, then hunkered down next to the stove.

Class, he mused. Sara had class. It had taken a bite of her pride to acknowledge that she'd been wrong about Moses, but she'd done it. He'd seen men simply glare at Moses when the older man outshined them. Yes, Sara Ann Calhoun had class.

"Gentlemen," Sara said, "did you cut any sign?"

"Nothing," Gabe said. "Didn't spot a thing."

Chuck, Ben and Billy shook their heads in the negative.

"Yep," Moses said.

Everyone looked at him.

"I found a field-stripped cigarette butt in the duff beneath a big old tree where the snow hadn't gotten all the way in. The tobacco was Bull Durham and fresh enough. Hux was staying on the center terrain to a hundred yards below this ledge. If we spread out from here up, we're okay. We didn't miss them below."

"You found tobacco particles in the duff, the debris beneath a tree?" Sara said, an incredulous tone to her voice. "How in the world did you do that?"

Moses shrugged. "I was looking for it."

Sara smiled and shook her head. As she took another sip of the hot, delicious chocolate, her eyes met Gabe's above the rim of the mug. He was looking directly at her, a slight smile on his face. He nodded once, very slowly, and she felt a rush of pleasure as she realized he was making it clear that he approved of her interchange with Moses, which had given the older man the respect due him.

In the next instant, she tore her gaze from his and stared into the mug.

She was being ridiculous again, she admonished herself. It made no difference to her whether she did, or did not, pass Gabriel Porter's approval. This was a Search and Rescue mission, not a social outing where seduction was the ultimate goal.

So, fine, Moses was a real asset to the team, and she'd acknowledged that fact. She was, however, still dealing with a volunteer unit who could not possibly have the extensive training she did. She was in charge, and it was time to move on.

She drained her mug, but before she could tell the others that the rest break was over, a chilling wind whipped along the ledge, accompanied by a dark shadow.

She looked up to see heavy clouds moving rapidly across the heavens.

"Here she comes," Moses said, scanning the sky.

At the moment Moses stopped speaking, snow began to fall heavily, as though a trapdoor had suddenly been opened. Everyone got to their feet, and Moses set about the task of dismantling the little stove.

"We'll switch to the buddy system," Sara said, handing her mug to Moses. "Two by two. I don't want anyone lost if it goes to whiteout conditions. You've seen the map of the terrain. We'll cover three of the waterways that flow down from the top. That's where wild game would go, and it's the best we can do."

"Right," Gabe said. "Moses, you're with Billy. Chuck with Ben. Sara, you and I will pair up."

Damn it, she thought. Gabe had no business giving orders. *She* would decide how the unit would divide. But... all right, he knew his men, the strengths and weaknesses of each, and she didn't. She did not, however, like the idea of being Gabe's partner.

Why? Oh, forget it. She wasn't going to waste precious time and energy thinking about it.

"Let's get started," she said. "The Huxleys are out here somewhere, and this new storm isn't going to make it any easier to find them. The temperature is dropping, and they're not wearing clothing that can maintain their body heat. I want radio check-ins from you every fifteen minutes."

"Roger," Ben said.

Sara assigned Moses and Billy the far left waterway, Chuck and Ben the one in the center, and told Gabe they'd take the far right. Everyone nodded in understanding, they checked to be certain their radios were sending and receiving, then started upward.

The snow was falling faster and thicker, and the wind was increasing, swirling the snow into stinging pellets. Radio contact was made after fifteen minutes. The pairs were moving slowly, there had been no evidence of the Huxleys being in any of the areas.

Sara and Gabe trekked on, not attempting to speak as they concentrated on where they were going and what was around them. Sara's lungs burned from inhaling the bitter cold air, and her legs ached from plodding through the deepening snow.

Radio contact was made again, although the static had increased and it was difficult to communicate.

The intensity of the snowfall and wind increased even more.

Suddenly Sara stopped and looked quickly around. She couldn't see Gabe!

He had been next to her, not more than two feet away, and now he was gone!

A flash of panic swept through her, and despite the freezing temperature, she felt dots of perspiration on her forehead. She couldn't see more than a few inches in front of her.

The storm had produced a full-fledged whiteout condition.

The vivid memory of her nightmare slammed against Sara's mind, causing a whimper to escape from her throat.

There was snow everywhere, in all directions. She was alone, enclosed within terrifying white walls, and it was cold, so very cold. She had to keep moving, but she couldn't see. Oh, dear God, where was Gabe?

"Gabe, where are you?" she shouted, the wind flinging her plea aside. "Gabe?"

"Sara," he answered, from beyond the wall of white. "Keep yelling my name. Don't move."

"Gabe...Gabe..." She swallowed a sob and forced strength into her voice. "Gabe!"

He suddenly appeared, seeming to burst through the white wall like a charging gladiator. He flung his arms around her and pulled her to him. She clung to him, relishing his size, the strength and power of his massive body, the very essence of him, and the knowledge that he was there. She was no longer alone.

"Whiteout," he said, having to raise his voice to be heard above the howling wind. "We've got to take shelter right away."

"The Huxleys..."

"We can't find them in this. You know that, Sara. My men will be staying put until this passes through, and so will we. We're on a flat enough stretch to set up my tent. Don't move, not one damn inch."

"But...I—"

"We're going to be just fine. Whiteouts are not fun and games, but we'll be all right. Sara, look, I...ah, hell."

Gabe shifted his hands to her shoulders, tightened his hold, then lowered his head and kissed her. The kiss was searing, rough, and heat and desire rocketed through Sara. He released her abruptly seconds later, causing her to stagger slightly.

"Don't move," he repeated, then disappeared once again into the whiteness.

Sara wrapped her hands around her elbows, then drew a steadying breath. Closing her eyes, she savored the lingering taste and feel of Gabe's lips on hers, as well as the sensations still simmering within her.

In the next instant, her eyes flew open again, and she blinked against the stinging snow.

The nerve of that man, she fumed. He'd just hauled her to him and kissed the living daylights out of her without so much as a by-your-leave. Gabriel Porter was arrogant, cocky and rude. *Extremely* rude.

Gabriel Porter also kissed like a dream, and if he hadn't stopped kissing her when he did, she probably would have melted into a puddle and been covered with snow.

Oh, Sara, shut up. It was a kiss for heaven's sake. No big deal. She was overreacting because of her temporarily frazzled state of mind.

The wind increased even more and she shivered, despite the weatherproof clothing she wore.

This was like a science fiction movie, she thought giddily. Gabe was being transported through time warps... here, then poof... gone.

Lord, this was frightening. They'd studied whiteout procedures at the academy, gone over and over the dangers of becoming disoriented, the importance of not moving unless you were positive you knew exactly where you were.

But she'd been taught nothing to prepare her for the fear, the feeling of helplessness, the horrifying image of being the only person left on the face of the earth.

She had to calm down, get herself under control. Gabe was functioning in an efficient I-know-what-to-do-and-I'm-doing-it manner, while she was behaving like a scared kid. She was watching her position of Incident Commander being taken over by Gabe, and it was entirely her fault.

Well, enough of this. Gabe had witnessed her fright as she'd clung to him like a lifeline, but that was *all* he would see. She would get herself back in control as quickly as she could, but until she was once again totally calm, she'd fake it.

And she would proceed as though the kiss they'd shared had never taken place.

Fine. No problem. But, oh, saints above, she wished he'd hurry so she'd no longer be alone in the midst of her nightmare.

Gabe worked by rote as he set up the tent. He'd been in whiteout conditions on two previous occasions and knew the dangers the situation presented.

When he'd first trained for Search and Rescue operations, he'd spent many hours blindfolded while practicing setting up the tent. The drill had held him in good stead before, and was making it possible for him to accomplish his goal now. He couldn't see more than inches in front of him as the velocity of the storm increased.

It would take him no more than ten to twelve minutes, he knew, to have the tent up and firmly secured with four poles. Then he could bring Sara to a place that was warm, dry and safe.

Sara, his mind hummed. Sara Ann Calhoun. He sure as hell hadn't intended to kiss her, he'd just suddenly done it. She'd looked so scared, like a frightened doe with great big eyes. He'd been incredibly aware of his masculinity, of the fact that he possessed the means to quiet her fears.

Why he'd kissed her, he didn't know, but it had been a sensational kiss that she'd totally responded to. Desire had exploded within him, flinging him instantly to the edge of his control. He definitely wanted to kiss Sara again. To be more precise, he definitely wanted Sara.

That's great, Porter, he thought dryly. He was in the middle of a Search and Rescue mission in a beaut of a whiteout, and he was thinking about making love with his Incident Commander. His brain must have frozen.

He moved around the tent for a final inspection, making certain the oval-shaped mound was taut and steady. It was seven feet long at the bottom, and would have five feet of room inside, with a height of three feet. It was bright yellow, but the cheerful color was already stark white with snow. The heavy-duty nylon floor would provide a dry surface to sit on.

"Home sweet home," he muttered.

He slid his pack inside the tent, secured the flap, then started back to get Sara.

As Gabe once again appeared in front of her, Sara stifled a near sob of relief.

"Come on," he shouted, taking her arm. "We have a room reserved at a five-star hotel."

Two minutes later, Gabe placed one hand on the back of Sara's head to bend her over, and she found herself propelled inside the tent. She sank to her knees and took off her backpack. Gabe fastened the flap, and the howling wind became a muffled noise in the distance.

"Take off your outerwear," Gabe said. "We'll spread it out as best we can at the end there."

Sara busied herself doing as Gabe had instructed, attempting to give the impression she was casually tending to undoing the snaps along the sides of her pants.

In actuality, she was scrambling for control, frantically trying to still the lingering fear and near-panic she'd experienced in the snow. She was so close to bursting into tears that she could feel an ache throbbing in her throat.

If Gabe noticed the trembling of her hands he would, she fervently hoped, surmise that she was chilled through. She was going to appear calm, cool and collected, even if it killed her. The Incident Commander of this mission was *not* announcing that she was quaking with terror.

She spread out the pants and top, and unzipped the heavy jacket to reveal her uniform blouse. She folded her legs Indian style, then glanced around.

"This is a top-notch high-altitude tent," she said. Had her voice betrayed her? It sounded strange to her own ears, very shaky and high-pitched. "I'm impressed."

Gabe stretched his long legs out in front of him, crossed them at the ankle and propped himself on his elbows. He looked at Sara intently.

She was putting on a facade of being laid-back, totally calm, he mused, but it wasn't working. Her hands and voice were shaking, there was still fear in those incredible green eyes of hers, and she was as white as the snow that had scared her so badly.

Obviously she didn't intend to confide in him one iota. So, all right, he'd respect that. For some unknown reason, though, he wished she'd talk it through, share her thoughts with him about how she'd felt in the whiteout, trust him enough to admit that she'd been terribly frightened.

"It's an excellent piece of equipment," he said, looking around the tent. He met her gaze again. "I spent a lot of time investigating makes and models before I finally bought this one."

"Where did you train for Search and Rescue?"

"With the Yavapai County Back Country Unit. They're the best in the state, in my opinion. Then I trained Chuck, Billy and Moses. There were three others early on, but they couldn't cut it." He sat up and reached for his radio. "This is useless but..." He pressed a button and produced crackling static. "Nope."

He put the radio on the nylon floor and settled back on his elbows. "Are you comfortable, Sara? We're going to be here a while, and it's a chance to rest. There's room for you to stretch out here next to me."

"No," she said quickly. "I mean, I'm fine right here." Stretch out next to Gabriel Porter like two peas in a pod? Not in this lifetime. Did he think she was a naive idiot? "I'm dandy."

"I'm not going to jump your bones, you know," he said, smiling.

"It never occurred to me," she said stiffly, picking an imaginary thread off her knee.

"Mmm," he said. "Well, I'm glad you consider yourself safe with me. We're all alone, just the two of us, cut off from the world. That's how I always feel when I'm in this tent. There's a sort of other-world atmosphere as though I've been transported to another time and place. I like it. It gives me a chance to get in touch with myself, make sure I'm hitting on all cylinders, staying on the right track. It's peaceful."

"Yes," Sara said slowly, "I guess it is. I know the storm is raging out there, but it suddenly seems very far away."

"Yep."

"An other-world atmosphere," she said softly, sweeping her eyes over the expanse again. She met Gabe's gaze. "Yes."

Neither spoke further as they looked directly into each other's eyes. Heartbeats quickened as the memory of the kiss they'd shared took precedence over other thoughts and images in their minds and mental visions. The tiny, glowing ember of desire that kiss had created within them grew brighter, hotter, threatening to burst into a raging flame of passion.

Lord, Gabe thought, how he wanted this woman. Sara Ann Calhoun was turning him inside out. He'd told her that when he was in this tent, he used the time for a personal inventory, making certain he was keeping himself, his life, on the right track, where he'd learned he belonged.

Learned? That was a very lightweight word to use, considering what he'd gone through to get from where he'd been to where he was now. There was nothing, *nor anyone,* capable of pulling him from the path he now walked.

So slow down, Porter, he told himself, *in regard to Incident Commander Calhoun.* He needed to discover much more about who she was, what made her tick, what her dreams and goals were.

"Sara," he said, breaking the sensuous spell that had woven around them, "what secret fantasy did you have when you were a kid?"

"A baby doll," she said, then stiffened, a flush of embarrassment staining her cheeks.

Dear heaven, she hadn't meant to say that. Gabe had caught her off guard while she'd been in a hazy sensual mist, captured in an invisible web and mesmerized by the dark depths of his eyes.

"Tell me about your baby doll," he said, his voice low and his gaze steady.

"No, I...no. It's silly. I haven't thought about that doll in nearly twenty years. I have no idea why it popped into my mind now."

Gabe shifted his arms, linking his fingers beneath his head on the nylon floor but making certain he was still able to see Sara clearly.

"It's this tent," he said, "the other-world aura in here. It transports you where you wish to go. You traveled way back in time and found your baby doll. What was her name?"

"Rosalie."

"Pretty. What did she look like, your Rosalie?"

"She wasn't mine. You said 'secret fantasy,' and it triggered the memory of my dream of having a baby doll named Rosalie. She'd have yellow curly hair, blue eyes that closed when I laid her down, and a lavender organdy dress. She... Gabe, this is ridiculous."

"No, it isn't. Why wasn't Rosalie yours?"

"My father raised me because my mother... was gone. We were a team, my dad and I, and we did just fine." She nodded. "Just fine. But, well, he gave me birthday and Christmas presents that he could relate to. You know, a baseball mitt, a bat, a cowboy hat, things like that."

Gabe smiled. "But you wanted a baby doll."

"Oh, yes," she said, a wistful tone to her voice. "I created Rosalie in my mind. There wasn't a doll that special in any store in Autumn. I'd lie in bed, pretend I was opening a box, brushing back the tissue, and there she'd be. Rosalie. So beautiful."

"Couldn't you have told your father how much you wanted a doll?"

She shook her head. "It would have hurt his feelings to think he'd disappointed me with the gifts he'd chosen. No, I couldn't tell him, or anyone. In time, I simply forgot about it."

"Until now."

"Yes, and I still say it's silly that it came to mind all these years later." She cleared her throat. "Gabe, I'd appreciate it if you'd forget we had this nonsensical conversation. I feel foolish having rambled on about a doll I never even owned."

Gabe looked at her for a long moment before he spoke.

"And the kiss we shared, Sara? Do you plan to forget that, too?"

Chapter Six

An amalgam of emotions tumbled together within Sara, then rose to the surface, rendering her momentarily speechless. Anger was present among the maze, and she mentally grabbed hold of it, clinging tightly, flinging the other emotions away with a sharp shake of her head.

"The kiss we *shared,* Mr. Porter?" she said, her voice rising. "You have a selective memory, mister. *You* kissed *me.* There was nothing *shared* about it."

Gabe came up off the floor to a sitting position so quickly that Sara flinched from the sudden, unexpected motion. He drew his knees up, then gripped them with his large hands.

"Now wait just a damn minute here," he said, none too quietly. "*You're* the one with the fuzzy memory. You responded to that kiss, lady. You gave as much as you took. That kiss, by damn, was *shared*."

Sara opened her mouth to retort, then snapped it closed in the next instant. She narrowed her eyes and looked at Gabe, her fingers drumming an uneven tempo on her bent knees as she reined in her temper.

"All right," she said finally, a tight edge to her voice, "I concede. Your point, Mr. Porter."

"I should hope so."

"However," she rushed on. She pointed one finger in the air. "The circumstances surrounding the said kiss must be addressed. It was a tense and unusual moment, with emotions running amok."

"Emotions running amok?" he repeated with a burst of laughter. "I can't believe you actually said that." He grinned and shook his head. "Running amok. Lord."

"Gabriel," Sara said, "shut up." She folded her arms over her breasts and stared straight ahead.

Gabe's smile slowly faded as he looked at her.

Sensational, he mused. Sara Calhoun angry was dynamite. Her eyes had been like green laser beams, and the pink flush on her cheeks a lovely contrast to her dark, silky hair. He wanted to kiss her again. Now. Right now. But since he was fond of living, he'd put the urge on hold. Temporarily.

"You know," he said quietly, "you've got some heavy-duty walls built around you, Sara. We're talking about a kiss. One kiss. One *shared* kiss. Yet, you're acting as though you've been very threatened by something. It's not as if we tore off our clothes and made mad, passionate love in a snowdrift."

Sara glared at him.

"Sara, you've scrambled behind those walls of yours that are so thick they're nearly tangible. Why? What are you afraid of?"

"Nothing. I'm not afraid of anything, Gabriel Porter. This absurd conversation is closed. And, yes, the kiss is forgotten. Understand? We're on a Search and Rescue mission. I'm the Incident Commander. You and your men are volunteers, which does nothing for my peace of mind."

She shook her head.

"I hope to the heavens that the Huxleys don't suffer the same consequences from having their lives in the hands of volunteers as..." She paused. "Never mind. Just forget it."

"No way. Not a chance. You're hitting me where I live with a real cheap shot. My unit is one of the best in the state. I will—hell, I have—staked my life on that fact. Who suffered from a volunteer unit? Come on, Sara, who are you talking about?"

"My father! Three years ago during the first December snow, he went hunting and was overdue coming in. Then here they came, the glory boys, strutting their stuff, ready to save the day. Volunteers. Oh, they thought they were so macho, heroes to the rescue."

She drew a shuddering breath and blinked away unwelcome tears.

"But they were totally inept, missed a sign that was right in front of them. They'd spent more time talking about being Search and Rescue hotshots than training to be a competent unit. Because of them, *my father died!*"

"Holy hell," Gabe whispered.

"I vowed that would never happen again, not in Canyon County." Two tears slid down her pale cheeks. "I went to Colorado, worked hard to obtain the training I needed, and now I'm back. I don't want you on this mission, Gabe. Not you, or your men, but I'm stuck with all of you, with volunteers."

"Who are doing a damn good job," he said, a muscle ticking in his jaw.

"So far. Yes, so far your unit is performing well, but this mission isn't over yet, because the Huxleys are still out there somewhere. We don't quit...do you understand me? We don't quit until we find them.

"That's all I care about. That's all that's important to me. My focus is on *this* mission, and the one after this, and the next, and the next. I don't have room in my life for anything other than the goals I set for myself three years ago."

Gabe nodded slowly. "Well, that's clear enough. You're dedicated to your career. End of story. I'm sorry about your father, Sara. That explains why Martha Broffy said what she did about this mission being difficult for you. I heard about that other unit, and I know they were disbanded.

"What you just told me explains the walls you have around you, but only to a point. So, okay, you don't want to be pulled off your career course, but I sense, I don't know, I just feel, there's more going on here. What else are you afraid of? Talk to me, Sara."

"I'm finished talking to you," she said, a weary quality to her voice. "I've said more than I ever intended to."

"Sara..."

"Leave me alone, Gabe. I want to rest until we can get out of here and resume the search. Just leave me alone."

"Fine." He lay back down, lacing his hands beneath his head again.

Several minutes passed in silence, a heavy oppressive silence.

"I can't help wondering though," he said finally, his voice very low. "Do you know the difference between being alone and being lonely?"

Again, Sara opened her mouth to speak, then closed it in the next instant. She shook her head wearily, shifted her position to wrap her arms around bent legs and rested her forehead on her knees.

Enough, she told herself. Gabe was putting her through an emotional wringer, draining her to the point of exhaustion. He'd forced her to address so many issues that were difficult for her under the best of circumstances, let alone in the middle of a Search and Rescue mission.

Damn the man, he'd been the one to lecture her about the necessity of staying relaxed as possible to conserve energy. So, what did he do? He'd dragged her through an emotional jungle, which held ghosts from the past that had chipped away at her with dark, clawing tentacles.

Gabriel Porter had no right to invade her privacy, move into her space, then push her to the wall.

Do you know the difference between being alone and being lonely?

Shut up, shut up, she mentally yelled. She was forgetting, as of now, everything that had taken place within that tent, with the damnable *shared* kiss thrown in for good measure. She was in charge, in control and ready to continue performing with maximum expertise.

Gabriel Porter could go straight to hell.

Sara reached for her clothing that was spread out at the end of the tent.

"I'm going outside to check the weather conditions," she said.

Gabe sat up. "I'll go."

"I'm the Incident Commander." She pulled on her jacket, not looking at Gabe. "I give the orders. You stay here, I'm going out."

"Sara, look, I'm sorry. My timing was way off on some of the things we talked about. This wasn't the place. I should have waited until—"

She snapped her head around to glare at him, interrupting him in midsentence when she spoke.

"What you should have done is minded your own business, Mr. Porter."

Before Gabe could reply, the radios crackled, causing them both to reach for their own.

"Heaven One, this is Heaven Six. Over," a voice said from the walkie-talkie, midst a great deal of static.

"It's for you, Ms. Incident Commander," Gabe said, matching her glowering expression.

"Heaven Six," she said into the radio's speaker, "this is Heaven One. Over."

"Moses here. The storm has passed through enough for us to get moving. It's nasty out there, but we can handle it. Over."

"Roger," Sara said. "Heaven Three, check in. Over."

"Heaven Three here," Chuck said. "We're ready to roll. Over."

"Let's do it, gentlemen. Over and out."

Sara finished snapping her outerwear into place, then reached for her backpack. Without looking at Gabe, or speaking to him, she left the tent.

Outside, she stood perfectly still, her gaze sweeping over the terrain in all directions. There was still a light snow falling, and the wind continued to blow, but Moses had been right... they could handle it.

It would be slow going, she knew, as the added inches of snow on the ground were wet and heavy.

Under different circumstances, Thinker's Thumb would be a spectacle of beauty. The snow was untouched and pristine white, and the tall pine trees looked as though they'd been artistically frosted like cakes by Mother Nature.

With speed and expertise, Gabe dismantled the tent and stowed it in his backpack. Sara radioed down for a report from the deputy waiting at the base camp at the bottom of Thinker's Thumb. The Huxleys had not appeared there, he said, or at their house. Sara informed the deputy that the search unit was once again on the move and heading further up the mountain.

There, she thought, she'd covered all the necessary details that fell under her blanket of responsibility. What she would *not* do was think of anything other than the mission, the finding of the three Huxleys.

For the next hour, they moved upward, the pace snail-slow as the deep, wet snow pushed heavily against every step they took. Radio checks were made in fifteen-minute intervals, but there was still no sign of the lost hunters.

Sara's fatigue and frustration grew, and a cold knot of fear tightened in her stomach for the safety of the missing man and his sons. She *knew* they were somewhere on that mountain, but it was beginning to seem as though they'd disappeared into the thin high-altitude air.

"Lord," Gabe said finally, "my leg muscles are screaming for mercy. This is like trying to move through wet cement."

"I know," Sara said, breathing heavily. "I thought I was in good shape, but I'm beginning to wonder."

Gabe chuckled. "Sara, Sara, you shouldn't give me lead-ins like that. I'm duty bound to say there is absolutely nothing wrong with your shape."

"I see," she said, laughing. "Is that on page whatever of the macho manual?"

"Yep."

"I think they send the manual home with all newborn baby boys. I—" She suddenly quit speaking and halted in her tracks. "Gabe?"

He stopped and looked at her questioningly. "What is it?"

"Smoke. I smell smoke. I can't see anything but... Wait. There. Look up there, Gabe. It's a thin line of gray smoke."

"You're right," he said, reaching for his radio. "I still can't smell it, though. You've got a dandy nose there, Sara Ann. It's cute, too." He pressed the button on the walkie-talkie, then released it. "Sorry. You're the Incident Commander. It's your ball."

Sara pulled her own radio free. "I'll report this to the others, but not bring them into this sector yet. If the Huxleys built a fire that's smoldering, but they've moved on, we'll have lost precious time covering the other areas."

"Fancy that," Gabe said, smiling. "That's exactly how I would play this hand. You book jockeys aren't *all* bad, ma'am."

She matched his smile. "You volunteers aren't all bad, either, sir." She paused. "I guess."

Gabe whooped with laughter. After Sara spoke with the others, they started off with renewed energy born of hope that the faint gray thread of smoke would lead them to the missing hunters.

Twenty minutes later Gabe stopped, cupped his gloved hands around his mouth and yelled, "Huxleys! Hello... Huxleys!"

Sara held her breath as Gabe's voice faded into the wind.

Then...

"Yo!" a distance voice replied. "Huxleys here. Up here."

"Dear God," Sara whispered, tears misting her eyes, "thank you."

"Let's go get 'em," Gabe said, grinning. "Call in the troops, Ms. Calhoun. They're invited to this party."

Fifteen minutes later, Sara and Gabe came over the top of a rise with knee-deep snow and there, thirty feet in front of them, they saw Frank, Bobby and Mike Huxley huddled on the ground beneath an enormous pine tree.

A small fire burned before them, and in front of that the field-dressed carcass of a large elk. Sara and Gabe ran to where they sat.

"Howdy, Sara Ann," Hux said, smiling broadly. "Nice to see you, miss. Thing is, though, what took you so long?"

"Hux," Sara said, smiling, "I don't know whether to hug you or hit you."

"My dad took a fall and got a busted leg," Mike said, his voice quivering. "How you gonna get him off the Thumb, Miss Calhoun?"

Sara looked up at the clearing sky, then back to Mike.

"How would you like a ride in a helicopter?" she said.

"Hey, yeah," Bobby said, "that would be cool."

"On one condition," Hux said.

"Which is?" Gabe said.

"You make room for this elk," Hux said, still grinning. "We've earned every pound of this son of a gun."

"It's a deal," Gabe said.

Sara pressed the button on her radio. "Base camp, this is Heaven One. Over."

"Base camp. Go ahead, Heaven One. Over."

Sara looked directly at Gabe and he met her gaze directly.

"We're at Heaven's Gate," she said into the speaker. "The Huxleys have been found. Evacuation procedures are as follows..."

* * *

A short time later, Chuck, Ben, Billy and Moses arrived on the scene, and handshakes were exchanged all around.

"Yeah!" Billy said. "Elk steaks."

Moses looked at Sara. "You got yourself to Heaven's Gate in fine fashion."

"Amen, Moses," she said softly. "Amen."

Chapter Seven

Many hours later, Sara threw back the blankets on the bed with a jerk that gave evidence of her frustration at her inability to sleep.

She pulled on socks, slipped on the well-worn velour robe and stomped toward the kitchen, turning on lights as she went. Once there, she poured milk into a pan and stirred it absently over a low heat, a deep frown on her face.

She was exhausted, nearly numb with fatigue. It was her mind, she knew, that refused to let go of the events of the day and allow her to indulge in the hours of blessed sleep she so desperately needed.

The Search and Rescue mission had been a success, and for that she would be eternally grateful. Much of the credit belonged to Frank Huxley himself, who had instructed his sons to gather armloads of the dry duff beneath the multitude of pine trees to make blankets from Nature's bounty. That, combined with the fire they'd built, had kept them alive until they were found.

Evacuation had gone smoothly, but had taken a great deal of time to accomplish. Then, according to the code of the National Search and Rescue Association, Sara was responsible for retrieving all the lime-colored pieces of tape tied to the trees and bushes.

Gabe and the other members of his team had insisted on helping, knowing that a top-notch Back Country Unit did nothing to harm the natural environment. The tape was removed, scrap by scrap.

It had been a weary group that had arrived back at the sheriff's office. They were so tired, Sara now realized, her frown deepening, that she hadn't given one thought to holding a debriefing meeting to fill out the final mission-report papers.

"Wonderful job," she said, shaking her head in self-disgust.

She poured the warm milk into a mug, then carried it to the table to sink wearily onto a chair. Propping her elbows, she held the mug in both hands and took a sip of the smooth, delicious drink.

There was no alternative, she mused, but to contact Gabe and request that he return to Autumn to supply data for the report. In actuality, the entire team should be called back, but that was too much to ask.

As the leader of his unit, Gabe's input would have to suffice.

Gabe. Gabriel Porter of the town of Rio, Copper County, Arizona. Gabe, who had caused a maelstrom of emotions to assault her, emotions that were part of the reason she was unable to sleep.

Her wakefulness was also due to still being on an adrenaline high from the execution of the search, something she'd been warned about at the academy.

She took a deep swallow of milk, then set the mug on the table.

Do you know the difference between being alone and being lonely?

"Oh, no, you don't, Gabriel," Sara said aloud, getting to her feet. "No. Nope. No way."

She was *not* addressing that little number in the middle of the night. In fact, she was dismissing Gabe, the kiss they'd... all right, they'd *shared*... the remembrance of the desire that had been evoked within her, her idiotic revelation regarding the coveted baby doll, everything that had transpired between her and Gabe. Yes, she was dismissing it all from her mind.

She ran water in the mug, set it in the sink, then turned to leave the kitchen.

"Right," she said dryly.

She returned to bed, pulled the blankets up to her nose and willed the calming, warm milk to lull her to sleep. At last somnolence claimed her, but her slumber was plagued by dreams that caused her to toss and turn.

She was encased in the cold, white world of snow, trembling in fear. And Gabe was there, appearing, then disappearing, time and again, always, always, just beyond her reach.

When Sara arrived at the sheriff's office the next morning, she was greeted by the aroma of coffee.

"Morning, Sara Ann," Jeb said when she entered the office. "I decided you deserved to have coffee waiting for you this morning as a salute to your finding the Huxleys yesterday. Now, don't go and get comfy with the idea of the brew brewing when you get here. This is a one-time celebration thing."

Sara laughed. "You're all heart." She poured a mug of coffee and took a sip. "Oh, good grief, I'm celebrating by being poisoned."

"The kind thought was there," Jeb said, chuckling. "I never said it would be a gourmet delight."

Sara sank onto her chair with a weary sigh. "Point taken. Well, if this stuff doesn't kill me, maybe it will wake me up."

"You do look a tad gray around the edges, miss. You put in long, hard hours yesterday. I wouldn't have had any problem with your taking off today. You certainly earned it."

"I have unfinished business from the mission, Jeb. I didn't hold a debriefing so I could fill out the final report. I need to contact Gabe in Rio and ask him to come back over so I can get his input. As the Incident

Commander, I should have met with the entire team when we came in. I never even thought of it."

"That's understandable. You were mighty tired soldiers, one and all." He paused. "It would seem you worked well with Gabe and the others, despite the fact that they're volunteers."

Sara rolled a pencil back and forth on the desk top with one fingertip, averting her eyes from Jeb's.

"Yes, well," she said, "Gabe and his unit are well trained, and have excellent equipment, which is so important in adverse weather conditions. I, um, I told him that his team had done a fine job."

"Imagine that," Jeb said, smiling. "It's nice to know that even a creaky old lady like you can change her opinions."

Sara looked up and glared at him, then frowned in concern as she saw him rubbing his chest.

"What's wrong?" she said. "Do you have a pain in your chest?"

"Yep, it's indigestion. That has got to be the worst coffee that has ever been poured into a mug. Do you want Gabe's phone number?"

"I'll get it from you later. Dealing with Gabriel Porter first thing in the morning is not my idea of a good time."

"Sara Ann, you just admitted that you'd put aside your ideas of Gabe being one of those glory boys, as you call them. Now what's your problem?"

"Nothing," she said quickly. "I'm just crabby, out of sorts, because I'm tired. I'll call him in a bit. Jeb, you're still rubbing your chest. Are you positive that you're all right?"

"As well as anyone could be after drinking battery acid." He got to his feet. "I'm going over to the drugstore and get some antacid tablets. Hold down the fort, Sara Ann."

"Sure thing," she said absently, watching him leave the room.

Chest pains, she thought. Jeb was having severe enough chest pains to cause him to go in search of something he hoped would ease the discomfort. Maybe she should urge him to stop in and see Doc Hartman.

No, she was overreacting. Jeb was like another father to her, and the desire to protect him, to keep him safe, as she had been unable to do for her father was rising to the fore in disproportionate measures due in part to her fatigue. The coffee really *was* awful, and if she drank any more of it, she'd probably have indigestion herself.

She had also overreacted to the thought of talking to Gabe. She hadn't even come close to accomplishing her goal of erasing from her mind all personal remembrances from the hours spent with him.

The dreams she'd had certainly hadn't helped any. There Gabe had been, through the restless night, haunting, taunting her with his presence.

He'd also been, much to her annoyance, the first person she'd thought of when she'd awakened. He'd hovered close to her as she'd showered, dressed, had breakfast and driven to work.

And he was *still* there, in that room, smiling that devastating smile and causing frissons of heat to whisper through her.

At least there was a saving grace about the unsettling situation. Gabe lived over half an hour's drive away, which meant she wouldn't be bumping into him every other minute on the streets of Autumn.

Once she'd called him, arranged for the debriefing session, then held the meeting, that would be that. And she *would* call him... later. After that, she wouldn't see him again until the next Search and Rescue mission, at which time she would be fully prepared to be strictly business.

The young deputy on duty came to the door of the office and cleared his throat, bringing Sara from her reverie.

"Yes, Randy?" she said.

"Call just came in. There's a fender-bender out on the Old Mill Road. Nobody hurt, just tempers flaring, and the road is blocked."

"I'll go," she said, getting to her feet. Even as exhausted as she was, keeping busy held a much greater appeal than sitting there like a lump fending off persisting images and thoughts of Gabe. "Jeb went to the store, and should be back in a few minutes. You'd think people would know enough to drive with extra care in this kind of weather."

Randy shrugged. "Things could get boring around here if we didn't have our winter quota of fender-benders. I guess you had enough excitement yesterday to last you a while, though. The Huxleys were lucky to get off Thinker's Thumb alive."

"Hux used common sense, which gave us time to get to him and the boys."

Randy laughed. "And he got his elk, the bum. I didn't even get drawn to hunt one."

"And so it goes," Sara said, starting across the room. "Tell Jeb where I am."

"You bet. He went to the drugstore?"

Sara laughed as she left the office. "Yes, he was after something to repair the damage done by his own coffee."

The simple fender-bender, as Randy had called it, was a bit more complicated than Sara had expected. Neither vehicle could be driven one inch.

Autumn's only service station possessed Autumn's only tow truck, resulting in two slow trips into town. Sara stayed at the location of the accident, attempting to keep as warm as possible by alternating between sitting in the patrol car, and jogging up and down the snow-encrusted road.

It was midafternoon before she finally reentered the sheriff's building, with its delightfully warm and welcoming interior. She shrugged out of her jacket, went toward the office she shared with Jeb, then stopped statue still in the doorway.

Gabe Porter was sitting in her chair, his hands laced behind his head. His feet, clad in shabby cowboy boots, were propped on the top edge of her desk.

Sara's gaze flickered over him, missing no detail of his tall, strong body. Due to the angle of his arms, the faded blue western shirt he wore was straining against the broad expanse of his chest, and the taut muscles in his arms were clearly defined beneath the soft material. His faded jeans accentuated the long length of his powerful legs.

Gabe and Jeb were laughing, obviously having shared a story or joke that tickled their male fancy. Gabe's laughter was rich, deep and rumbling, his smile wide, the dimple in his cheek seeming to wink at her with sensual arrogance. His thick, dark hair was tousled, inviting her fingers to comb through it to restore a sense of order.

Gabriel Porter, Sara mused, was one hundred percent male, with a blatant masculine magnetism thrown in for good measure. She could feel the heat curling low within her, was acutely aware of her own femininity, *and* of Gabe's ability to throw her physically and emotionally off balance.

She wanted, she knew, to turn and run, leave the building before Gabe became aware of the fact that she had been there. She didn't want to talk to him, have him look directly at her with his mesmerizing dark eyes. She didn't want the ember of desire within her that couldn't be ignored to be fanned to a hotter flame that would threaten to consume her. Damn it, she didn't want Gabriel Porter to be there.

"Get your crummy boots off my desk, mister," she said, stomping into the room.

Gabe's head snapped around to look at her, and in the next instant, his feet hit the floor with a thud. He stood, took a handkerchief from his back pocket and scrubbed at the edge of the desk top.

"There you go," he said, grinning. "It's as good as new. You'd never know that I was here."

Oh, ha, Sara thought. He was there, all right. Good Lord, was he ever there.

"Thank you," she said coolly.

"Gabe came over to see you, Sara Ann," Jeb said. "He figured you'd want to have a debriefing so you could file a report on the Search and Rescue mission. I told him you were planning on calling him about that."

"Yes, of course, I was," she said, looking at Jeb rather than Gabe. "I've been tied up for hours with an accident on the Old Mill Road."

Jeb nodded. "Randy told me. That's more paperwork for you, writing up the accident report. Well, that can keep for now. Gabe is a busy man with a ranch to run, so I'd suggest you huddle up with him, and tend to the debriefing."

"Excellent idea," Gabe said. "Let's go huddle up, Sara."

She glared at him. "I'll gather the necessary forms, and meet you in the room down the hall."

He rocked slowly back and forth on the balls of his feet, his arms crossed loosely over his chest.

"No rush," he said pleasantly. "I'll wait here while you get what you need."

"Will you excuse me then?" she said. "You're standing in front of the desk drawer that I need to open."

"Oh, yes, ma'am," he said, coming from behind the desk. "Cooperation is my middle name."

Not even close, Sara thought. Dangerous was his middle name. He was exasperating, cocky and *very* dangerously exciting.

"Well," Jeb said, getting to his feet, "now that you're back, Sara Ann, I think I'll take a cruise around town and make sure everything is in order." He walked to the front of his desk. "I'll see you two when I..."

Jeb suddenly stopped speaking and clutched the front of his uniform shirt with both hands.

"God almighty," he said, gasping. "Martha? Martha, I..." He slumped heavily to the floor, then sprawled out, facedown.

"Jeb!" Sara yelled, rushing to him. She sank to her knees beside him. "Jeb? He's unconscious, Gabe."

Gabe dropped to one knee next to her and placed two fingertips on Jeb's neck.

"Pulse is thready," he said. "Looks like a heart attack."

"Oh, dear God," Sara said. "He said it was indigestion from the terrible coffee he made. He said...

Jeb? Come on, Jeb, open your eyes. Don't do this. Jeb?" Tears misted her eyes. "Please?"

No! her mind screamed. She couldn't lose Jeb, too. He and Martha were all she had left of the few she'd loved. Her mother and her beloved father were gone forever, and now Jeb was... Oh, God, no.

Gabe gripped her shoulders and turned her toward him with a small jerk.

"Get it together. Now," he said. "Emotions come later, Sara. Jeb needs action, not tears. I'll tell Randy to radio for an ambulance. You call Martha." He stood, hauling her to her feet in the process. "Move."

"Yes. Yes, I understand," she said, her voice unsteady. "Tell Randy to call Doc Hartman, too."

"Hartman. Got it." He sprinted from the room.

Sara snatched up the receiver to the telephone on Jeb's desk, dreading the moment that Martha Broffy would answer the ringing with a cheerful hello.

The small hospital where Jeb was taken was located halfway between Autumn and Rio. Built to service the citizens of both towns and the surrounding areas in Canyon and Copper Counties, it had been named Copper Canyon Regional Medical Center. Those who lived in the vicinity referred to it simply as Three C.

Sara, Martha and Gabe sat on lumpy leather chairs in the hospital's waiting room, each lost in their own thoughts. There had been a flurry of activity when they'd first arrived, but no one had spoken to them for the past, seemingly endless, hour.

Sara had managed, by sheer force of will, to push aside her own anguish over Jeb, and present as calm a facade as possible for Martha. The older woman had seemed so withdrawn. The silence in the small room was oppressive.

Sara finally got to her feet. "I'd better call into the office and make sure everything is under control and running smoothly there."

Gabe glanced at her and nodded. Martha gave no indication that she had heard Sara speak.

A few minutes later, Sara returned to the room and sat down in the chair next to Gabe.

"I spoke with Randy," she said quietly. "The three other deputies are out on calls. There's a four-car pileup near Thinker's Thumb, some drunk hunters are using Clem Shipman's barn for target practice, and another group of hunters have shot and killed two of Donny Harrison's milk cows. If another call comes in, Randy will contact me here, and I'll have to go."

"I can go," Gabe said.

"No, you can't. Arrests might have to be made. You don't have any authority to—"

Gabe held up one hand to silence her, then reached into his back pocket for his wallet. He withdrew a laminated card and handed it to Sara.

She read it quickly, then looked at him, surprise evident on her face.

"You're a deputy for both Copper and Canyon Counties?" she said.

He nodded. "Everyone in my Search and Rescue Unit is deputized. We've completed all the necessary training, and both Jeb and the Copper County sheriff authorized us to be card-carrying deputies."

"I didn't realize that could be done," Sara said, giving him back the card.

"Yep. Hunting season is trouble waiting to happen. As of now, you're the acting sheriff of Canyon County, and I'm one of your deputies. There's enough personnel in Copper County. You've got a case of the shorts, so consider me on duty as a member of your staff."

"But what about your ranch?"

"I'll have it covered with a phone call. I set it up that way from day one. I made up my mind when I left Los Angeles that I'd be in control of my life from then on, not have a job, career, whatever, controlling me. That's freedom to live, not just exist, and it's extremely important to me. Maybe you can't understand that, because you're so focused on your career."

Before Sara could reply, Martha got to her feet and went to the doorway of the room. She stopped, then turned to look at Sara and Gabe.

"It's been so long," Martha said, her voice trembling. "Surely they could tell us *something*. Of course, I do trust Doc Hartman. Heavenly days, he's been in Autumn forever, it seems.

"He helped bring you into this world, Sara Ann. I can remember him saying you arrived mad as blue blazes over being disturbed from your comfortable little world, and you hollered the roof down.

"I know Doc is taking fine care of my Jeb, it's just that..." She stopped speaking and shook her head, as emotions choked off her words.

Gabe got to his feet and went to her, wrapping his arms around her in a comforting hug.

"I know this waiting is tough, Martha," he said, "but you're not alone. Sara and I are right here with you. Doc Hartman will speak to you just as soon as he can."

Martha nodded and allowed Gabe to lead her back to her chair. She took a hankie from her purse and dabbed at her nose.

"Jeb would have a fit if he knew I was falling apart. He's always been so proud of me because I understood and accepted the dangers that went with his being sheriff. But this is different. A heart attack. I just... I just wasn't prepared for this."

"Of course you weren't," Sara said gently. "None of us were. Jeb is a fighter, Martha, you know that. He won't knuckle under and give up. He'll be spitting mad and demanding they let him out of this place. He'll be fine, you'll see."

"It's time he retired, Sara Ann," Martha said, her voice ringing with determination. "I've stood by him all these years, never knowing if they'd come to my door and say he'd been killed in the line of duty.

"Well, enough is enough. I love that ornery old buzzard, and I'll be damned if I'm going to spend the rest of my life alone because he refused to turn in his badge. He promised me we'd go on a cruise when he retired, and it's overdue. Sheriff Broffy is going to become private citizen Broffy, or he'll be dead in the ground because I will have shot him myself."

Gabe chuckled. "That's the spirit. Give him hell. You're thinking the same way I do, Martha. You've earned the right to have the freedom to control your life, your present and future. Leave the tunnel vision, the focus on career only, to people like Sara." He slid a glance at Sara. "Right, Sara Ann?"

"Well, I . . ." she started, then glared at him. "This is hardly the time or place to get into a debate over career goals."

Gabe shrugged. "I'm just chatting. I'm thoroughly agreeing with Martha, you realize, leaving you outnumbered two to one with your attitude, so you'd be at a disadvantage in a debate, anyway."

"Well, I'll have my say," Martha said. "Sara Ann, what's happened to Jeb should be a lesson to you. He hardly took a day off during all these years as sheriff. I should have dug in my heels and demanded he have a better balance in his life. Now? He may not get a chance to do all the things he talked about that were always put off for *later*. It would break my heart if you did that to yourself, Sara Ann. It truly would."

Sara opened her mouth to reply, but snapped it closed as she realized she had no idea what to say.

"Think about it," Gabe said, looking at her intently. "Think about it long and hard."

Chapter Eight

Doc Hartman appeared in the doorway a few minutes later. He was short and round, had receding gray hair, and a generally rumpled appearance that everyone in Autumn considered a given in regard to the doctor. No matter what time of day or night it might be, Doc Hartman always presented the picture of someone who had slept in his clothes.

The doctor crossed the room, kissed Martha on the cheek, told Sara she was too skinny, then shook Gabe's hand after Martha introduced the two men.

"Well," Doc said, "Jeb Broffy is a lucky man. He had a heart attack, all right, but it wasn't severe. He's going to live to beat me at gin rummy for a lot of years yet."

"Oh, thank God," Martha said, dashing two tears from her cheeks.

Sara nodded in agreement with Martha's emotionally spoken words. Sara's throat was momentarily choked with unshed tears, making it impossible for her to speak.

"Jeb will have to take it easy," Doc Hartman went on, "and he's on a strict diet as of right now."

"He's also going to retire," Martha said. "He'll be informed of that little tidbit just as soon as I get a chance to tell him."

"I know you, Martha Broffy," the doctor said, "when you get your mind set on something, man and beast best get out of your path if they like living."

"Indeed," she said, lifting her chin.

"May we see Jeb, Doc?" Sara said.

"Just Martha for now, and only for a few minutes. You can stop in tomorrow. I'm keeping him here for a couple of days at least, where I can make certain he does nothing but rest. Well, rest and play gin rummy. I'm in to him for thirty-two cents, and I plan to recoup my losses.

"Come on, Martha, I'll take you to him. Sara Ann, go eat something. You're skinny as a fence post. Nice meeting you, Gabe."

"My pleasure," Gabe said. He kissed Martha on the cheek. "I'm really glad things turned out all right, Martha. Go see your Jeb."

Sara and Gabe watched as Martha left the room with Doc Hartman.

Sara drew a wobbly breath, let it out slowly, then realized that her earlier fatigue had deepened to the point that she ached from head to toe.

She wrapped her hands around her elbows in an unconscious gesture of attempting to protect the last shreds of her energy.

"I wish I could have seen Jeb," she said softly, still staring at the empty doorway. "I wouldn't have disturbed him, I just need to *see* him, know he's really alive and..." She shook her head. "That's silly. Of course, he's alive. Doc Hartman told us that Jeb will be fine. Yes, Jeb Broffy is alive."

Gabe studied Sara as she spoke, a frown knitting his brows.

He couldn't be certain, he knew, but he had the impression that Sara wasn't aware that she was speaking aloud. He'd also bet that the need to actually see Jeb was intertwined with the death of her father. There was an edge of near-panic to her voice that he could hear despite the fact that she was talking hardly above a whisper.

She looked so lost and alone, vulnerable, as though she might shatter into a million pieces at the slightest provocation. Her face was pale, with dark smudges beneath her green eyes, which lacked their usual sparkle.

Ah, Sara, he thought. He wanted to scoop her up and carry her out of there, tell her she *wasn't* alone because, by damn, Gabriel Porter was there. He would soothe her fears, comfort her, hold her tightly in his arms while she slept, getting the rest she obviously needed.

And when she awoke, they'd make love, beautiful love, for hours. There'd be no world, no worries, nothing, beyond the place the two of them created together.

"Well," Sara said, snapping Gabe back to attention, "I'd better get to the office. As acting sheriff, I have responsibilities."

"Which include not falling on your face," Gabe said, surprised at the angry tone of his voice. "You're out on your feet, Sara. When did you eat last?"

"Eat?" she repeated, looking at him. "I had breakfast at home this morning, then..." She paused, frowning. "That's it, I guess."

Gabe gripped her elbow. "That settles it. We'll go have dinner right now."

"Wait a minute," she said, jerking her arm free. "Randy is probably alone at the office. I doubt if the other deputies are back in from the calls they went out on. They might need help out there, too. Drunken hunters are not always pleasant or easy to deal with. I can't think about eating dinner. I have—"

"Responsibilities," Gabe interjected. "Yes, I know. You're a broken record on the subject. We'll call Randy from here. If everything is under control, we'll inform him that Acting Sheriff Calhoun and Deputy Porter can be reached at the Autumn Leaves Restaurant three blocks from the office. Don't argue with me, Sara Ann. I'm not in the mood." He started across the room. "Come on."

She was *not,* Sara decided, moving one inch. How dare that arrogant so-and-so give her orders? She wouldn't go out to dinner with him if she was starving to death.

Then again, she *was* starving to death, and the Autumn Leaves had the biggest, juiciest steaks in Canyon County. She'd only be three blocks away if Randy needed her and...

"Sara!" Gabe yelled from the doorway.

She jerked, then glowered at him. "All right. I'll eat. But not because you're barking at me, Porter. It just so happens that I'm very hungry."

She marched to the door, then whizzed past him, her nose poked in the air.

A smile crept onto Gabe's face, then widened into a grin as he followed her.

Sensational, he mused. Sara Ann Calhoun was really something.

Autumn Leaves was a cozy family restaurant with a rustic country decor. Round wooden tables were flanked by captain's chairs with comfortable, puffy cushions on the seats.

No one rushed through their meal at the restaurant but, as Jeb had once told Sara, nobody he knew in Autumn had a hurry-up attitude about anything.

They called Randy from the hospital, and the deputy was relieved to hear the positive news on Jeb.

Randy was happy to report all calls were taken care of and everyone, he concluded, was on standby, as per the usual hunting season procedure. He would call Sara and Gabe at the restaurant if they were needed.

Gabe had looked so darn smug as Sara relayed the information to him, she refused to speak to him during the drive from the hospital back to Autumn.

In the restaurant, Sara's less-than-sunshine mood faded into oblivion as she took the first bite of the juicy steak set in front of her.

"Mmm," she said, closing her eyes for a moment. She chewed and swallowed. "Delicious."

"Yes, ma'am," Gabe said, nodding.

They ate in silence for a few minutes, taking the edge off their appetites as they consumed portions of fluffy baked potatoes dripping with butter and mounds of sour cream, and crisp, crunchy garden salads.

"Jeb mentioned that your father owned an antique store," Gabe said finally, "but that you'd liquidated the stock. The business didn't hold any appeal for you, I take it."

"No, not really. Besides, he didn't have an inventory of great worth. He sort of dabbled in it when the mood struck. I'm living in the house I grew up in, though. Jeb and Martha kept an eye on it while I was away. It's small, but it certainly fills my needs. My father and I were happy there after my mother..." Sara's voice trailed off.

"Your mother?" he prompted.

"Well, it's no secret in Autumn, it's just very old news. She walked out, left us, because she wanted more than her life here offered. I have only vague memories of her, because I was four years old when she left."

"That's rough."

Sara lifted one shoulder in a shrug. "Not really. I didn't have a mother long enough to miss *not* having one. Besides, I had Martha and Jeb."

"They're good people."

"Yes, and I'm so very grateful that Jeb is going to be all right. I love the Broffys. The thought of losing either of them is..." She shook her head. "At the hospital, I kept thinking of my father and...well, everything is fine so there's no sense in dwelling on it."

So, he'd been right, Gabe mused, taking another bite of steak. Sara *had* been hurled back in time by Jeb's illness. Her need to actually see Jeb alive made perfect sense. Patrick Calhoun had been dead when the Search and Rescue team reached him.

Sara's world of loving was very narrow, as far as he could determine. She'd loved her mother and father, and they were gone. She loved the Broffys, and had been terrified when Jeb had the heart attack.

Was there room, he wondered, in the space behind her walls for a man, a lover, a husband? Just how proficient was she at protecting herself against the risks of loving? Were *all* her emotional energies beyond what she felt for Martha and Jeb directed toward her career?

If that was the case, she was making a tremendous mistake. He'd walked that road, lived that kind of life, and the price tag was far too high.

"Are you planning on training a Search and Rescue Back Country Unit in Autumn?" he said.

Sara sighed. "I certainly hope so. None of Jeb's deputies were interested in my proposal, which was disappointing. Once things calm down, I intend to take a serious look at the possible candidates for a team made up of men and women in this area."

"If Martha gets Jeb to retire, which I have no doubt that she will, you'll be acting sheriff until the next election, don't forget. Where will you find the time to train green recruits for Search and Rescue?"

"Oh, I'll find the time. That is my main purpose for returning to Autumn. What happened to my father won't occur again in Canyon County."

"What about the flowers, Sara?"

"Pardon me?"

"The flowers. The ones you're not even considering stopping long enough to smell. I found out the hard way that those flowers are very important. My ex-wife and I were both career oriented to the max. One day we realized we really didn't know each other anymore. She's still pursuing her career full steam ahead. I decided to take control of my life. Thus, the ranch in Rio."

"To each his own," Sara said breezily. "Oh, I'm stuffed, but that was a superb dinner. I'm getting a second wind now that I've eaten." She smiled. "I'll concede the point to you, Mr. Porter. Having dinner was an excellent idea."

"Yep," he said, nodding absently.

Sara's walls, he thought dryly, did double duty. Trying to get through to her on an issue of importance was like talking to a solid brick wall.

"You must be eager to get on your way, Gabe," Sara said, bringing him back to attention. "The drive to Rio will be slow going due to the road conditions."

"I'm a temporary Canyon County deputy, remember? I'm not going back to Rio tonight."

"But you don't have clothes, shaving gear, what have you. Tomorrow is certainly soon enough for you to report to duty here."

"One of my men on the ranch is driving over with what I need. I imagine he's delivered it to Randy by now."

"Oh. Well, you're definitely organized."

"True, but only because I have the freedom to organize my life to a level that I want it. *I'm* in control."

"So you've said several times," she said, raising one eyebrow. "You do have a hint of a soapbox attitude on the subject. Just where do you plan to stay while you're in Autumn?"

Gabe leaned back in his chair, rubbed one hand over his chin, and frowned.

"Now that's a bit of a problem. The one motel here is booked solid with hunters. The jail cells are occupied, and they're not my idea of nifty accommodations, anyway. The last thing Martha needs at the moment is someone bunking in her guest room. She'd insist on cooking huge meals for me, and she has enough to do because of Jeb."

"Well, you'll think of something."

"Yep. I already have."

"Oh?"

"Sure. One telephone call can produce two law enforcement officers. That's very efficient."

"I'm not following you."

"It's very simple, Sara," he said, an expression of pure innocence on his face. "I'm going to stay with you at your house."

Chapter Nine

Sara blinked, opened her mouth, shut it again, then shook her head slightly. In the next instant, she narrowed her eyes and leaned toward Gabe.

"You are out of your mind," she said.

"Why? It's a great idea. Like I said, it's extremely efficient."

"It's totally insane. Autumn is a small town, you yo-yo, and the gossips would have a field day with the juicy tidbit that Gabriel Porter is staying with Sara Calhoun, just the two of them."

"Sara, Sara," he said, shaking his head. "You're underestimating the citizens of this fair burg. Surely they're as laid-back and easygoing as the folks in Rio. No one passes judgment on anyone else.

"When the word gets out about Jeb, and it's made clear that I'm here to assist you, the acting sheriff, during the crisis, I can't believe that eyebrows will be raised."

Sara drummed the fingers of one hand on the top of the table as she weighed and measured Gabe's argument for his proposed plan.

His reasoning was sound, she admitted. The people in Autumn were open-minded and fair, having the attitude that everyone was free to live as they chose with no censure passed as long as the individual's actions did not hurt or harm anyone else.

Folks would, in fact, frown in concern if Gabe stayed with Martha Broffy. She would, everyone knew, cluck and fuss over a houseguest, and insist on preparing him three square meals a day. Martha's energies needed to be directed toward Jeb, not on someone bunking in her spare bedroom.

Darn it, Sara inwardly fumed, she had no solid case to present against Gabe's plan. The citizens of Autumn would accept the situation, no questions asked.

The knot in her stomach that had formed as she envisioned Gabe staying in her small house was due to *her* personal misgivings. They would have to share one bathroom, sleep in rooms separated by a scant few feet, sit across the breakfast table from each other.

Not good. Not good at all. She was experiencing enough difficulty keeping sane around Gabe Porter without living under the same roof with him. But what choice did she have? With Jeb out of commission, and the hunters out in full force, she needed Gabe's help to maintain order in Autumn.

Sara sighed and threw up her hands in defeat. "All right, you win, Gabe. You can stay at my house. Let's go tell Randy the plan, and make certain it's clearly written out for the shift changes."

Gabe nodded, then signaled to the waitress for the check.

Bingo, he thought, suppressing a smile. He'd done it. Luckily for him, Sara seemed to have completely forgotten that he owned a top-notch tent that he could have camped in with reasonable comfort. He was about to take up temporary residence in Sara's house. Excellent.

Why had he been so determined to accomplish that goal? he asked himself. His motive was not seduction, although he admittedly wanted Sara. Oh, yes, he certainly did, and the mere thought of making love with Sara caused heat to rocket through his body.

But, no, that wasn't his intention. Sara intrigued him, as well as unsettled him. He'd been unable to push her from his thoughts.

There were so many layers to her, such depth, that he'd had quick glimpses of when she'd lowered her damnable protective walls. Then she'd smacked those walls back into place and revealed nothing more than a career-oriented woman with tunnel vision regarding her goals.

She'd dismissed his reference to her need to stop and smell the flowers as unimportant. Well, he knew differently, had paid a heavy price for living out the attitude Sara possessed. Somehow, he had to get through to her, make her realize she was on a destruction course.

Do-gooder Porter, he thought dryly. He was hellbent on saving Sara from herself. True. But to be perfectly honest with himself, he also wanted to get to know her better, determine why she'd had such an impact on him. Sara Ann Calhoun was the cause of many questions plaguing him and he, by damn, wanted the answers.

Gabe insisted on paying for dinner, Sara thanked him politely, and they left the restaurant.

At the sheriff's office, Randy accepted Sara's announcement of where she and Gabe could be reached as casually as he might her saying she was going out to buy a doughnut. Randy wrote down the information for the deputies on the next shifts, then told Gabe that his gear had been delivered and was in Sara's and Jeb's office.

Gabe said he'd follow Sara home in his own vehicle, and much sooner than she was prepared for, they were standing in her living room.

"Very nice," Gabe said, his gaze sweeping over the area. "Cozy. Homey. I can see why you decided to keep this house. No, correct that. It's a home, has that special feeling of wrapping itself around you and saying welcome."

Sara tilted her head slightly to one side as she looked up at him, a rather bemused expression on her face.

"Thank you," she said. "That's how *I* feel about it, but I didn't think men noticed such things."

"Some men don't. *I* do. After my divorce, I mentally roamed the rooms of the large apartment where my ex-wife and I had lived. It was expensively furnished, had been decorated by a prestigious firm in Los Angeles. It was showroom perfect. But it was cold, appeared as though no one lived there. There were no personal touches, not one thing to give a clue as to who we were."

He swept one arm through the air.

"This room has personality, would tell wonderful stories if it could talk. I like your home, Sara, very much." He nodded, then met her gaze. "It suits you. Thank you for allowing me to share it with you."

"You're welcome," she said softly, unable to tear her gaze from his.

Oh, dear, she thought, the man just didn't quit. On top of everything else she was having such difficulty dealing with in regard to Gabe, he had sensed, felt, the same warmth and welcome in her shabby little home as she did. She really wished he'd stay in his arrogant mode and quit revealing an endearing sensitivity.

"Well," she said, a little too loudly, "I'll show you to your room. I imagine you're exhausted, so don't feel you have to stay up and engage in idle conversation with me to be a polite guest. Oh my, no, that isn't necessary."

Blast, Sara inwardly fumed, she was babbling, making a complete fool of herself.

"Follow me," she mumbled, then hurried across the living room, turning on more lights as she went.

In the bedroom that had been her father's, Sara flicked the wall switch to bring alive small lamps on mismatched end tables on either side of the double bed.

"This is it," she said. "Nothing fancy. There are clean towels in the cabinet in the bathroom. We'll have to work out a schedule, I guess, for morning showers. Okay? Sure. Good night, Gabe."

Gabe set his canvas sports bag on the floor, then straightened to look directly into Sara's eyes.

"Do I make you nervous, Sara?" he said, his voice very low.

"Nervous? Me?" she said, splaying one hand on her chest. "Don't be silly. Why would you think that you make me nervous?"

"Oh, I don't know," he said, lifting one shoulder in a shrug. "Maybe because you're as attracted to me as I am to you. Maybe because you can't forget that kiss we shared on Thinker's Thumb, any more than I can. Maybe because you're aware, very aware, that we're here alone, just the two of us."

Heat skittered along Sara's spine, then swirled into a pulsing warmth deep within her.

Gabe was batting a thousand, she thought. He'd gotten three out of three correct, right smack on the money. But if he thought she was going to admit to any of them, he was crazy.

She crossed her arms tightly over her breasts. "Your tiny mind is at work again, Porter. We've established the fact that your staying here is the best solution to the housing problem in Autumn. But it's strictly business. And I am *not* nervous. I'm exhausted, that's what I am. I'm going to take a bubble bath, then go to bed. If you shower in the morning, that will solve the traffic jam in the bathroom. End of story."

"I see," he said, a slow grin inching onto his lips. "Would it be an imposition if I stayed up awhile? I'm really not tired."

"Oh, well, fine, no problem. Feel free to light a fire in the fireplace if you like. Bye." She spun around and left the room.

Gabe watched her go, the smile broadening into a grin. He picked up the sports bag, set it on the bed, then began to hang his clothes in the small closet.

He shouldn't have taunted Sara about her nervous state, he supposed, but she'd been so flustered, and looked so adorable because of it, he couldn't resist.

He'd better shape up, he thought, chuckling softly, or he was liable to find himself booted out the door into a snowdrift.

A short time later, Gabe heard water running in the bathroom as he busied himself preparing a fire in the hearth. He settled onto the rather lumpy sofa and watched the leaping flames.

Sara was taking a bubble bath. Her cheeks were probably flushed from the steamy heat in the bathroom, her silky, curly hair slightly damp. She'd skim a soapy washcloth over her satiny skin as bubbles clung enticingly to her breasts and...

He muttered an earthy expletive as his body reacted to the sensuous scenario he was envisioning in his mind's eye. He shifted on the couch, then snatched up a magazine from the coffee table.

After attempting and failing to concentrate on an article about mountain climbing, he tossed the magazine back onto the pile, spread his arms along the top of the sofa and glowered at the dancing flames of the fire.

Sara savored the soothing warmth of the water in the tub and inhaled the delicate aroma of lilacs produced by the billowing mounds of bubbles.

With a weary sigh, she slid lower into the water, stopping when the bubbles touched her chin. Leaning her head back against the tiled wall, she closed her eyes.

Gabe's words spoken about the welcoming aura of her home echoed in her mind.

"Sensitivity," she whispered.

He'd shown the same type of sensitivity toward Mavis Huxley. He'd somehow known what Mavis needed to hear, despite the fact that Mavis knew it wasn't a guaranteed promise.

Sara sighed again.

She'd hammered away at Mavis, intent on gathering as much information as quickly as possible. That was what she'd been trained to do at the academy, but the human element had been missing. The sensitivity.

Oh, she had so much to learn in so many areas to gain the level of expertise she needed to achieve her goals in Search and Rescue work. And she was so very tired, thoroughly discouraged. She wanted to indulge in a long, loud cry, adding tears for her beloved Jeb.

No tears tonight, Sara Ann, she told herself firmly. She wasn't about to entertain Mr. Gabriel Porter by wailing her little heart out. He'd probably come dashing through the door, in a typical macho response, to rescue her from whatever was causing her dismay.

There he'd be, towering above her bed of bubbles, demanding to know where the dragons were hiding so he could slay them.

She would open her eyes slowly to meet his gaze, then ease herself upward, the water sluicing over her like satin ribbons, lilac-scented bubbles decorating her body like fairy-made frosting. Gabe would lift her into his arms, not caring that his clothes were becoming soaked, not caring about anything except her.

His lips, yes, those delectable lips, would claim hers in a searing, passionate kiss, which she would return in wanton abandon, then...

Sara opened her eyes and sat bolt upright so quickly that bubbly water splashed over the edge of the tub onto the floor. Good grief, she thought, *wanton* was the applicable word, all right, for her wayward mind. She'd never in her life had sexual fantasies.

Of their own volition it seemed, her fingertips drifted upward to rest lightly on her lips, the remembrance of the kiss shared with Gabe on the mountain haunting her once again. The taste, the feel of his mouth on hers was so vivid in her memory it was as though he were kissing her at that very moment.

She dropped her hands and snapped her head around to stare at the closed door, having the irrational thought that Gabe would somehow sense, know, where her mind had traveled to.

What was Gabe Porter doing to her? she wondered, with a rush of panic. She'd been surrounded by men as she'd taken courses in law enforcement, and again during the time at the Search and Rescue Academy. But none of them had flung her into such emotional confusion and sensual, physical reactions.

Gabe was dangerous, a threat to her purpose in life, her goals that she was determined to achieve. She must *not* allow his masculine magnetism to pull her off course like a helpless magnet under its power.

She was in close proximity to Gabe, and there was no help for it. She needed him performing in his role as deputy. But she could, and would, distance her mind from him, just shut down, not think, not feel.

She had to. Somehow.

Hours later, Sara registered a frustrating sense of déjà vu as she threw back the blankets on the bed and reached for her robe. Despite her bone-deep fatigue, she was unable to sleep and would once again try her warm milk remedy.

She opened the door to her bedroom very slowly and peered out, relieved to see no light creeping from beneath the closed door of Gabe's room. Moving cautiously, she went down the hall, then crossed the living room, using the glow of the embers in the hearth as light.

In the kitchen, she turned on only the small fluorescent bar above the sink, then began to prepare her drink in the dimly lit, shadowy room.

This was ridiculous, she fumed. She was skulking around in her own home like a thief in the night. However, this performance held greater appeal than the possibility of awakening Gabe and having him appear on the scene. She did *not* want a nocturnal visit from Mr. Porter.

After adjusting the low flame beneath the pan containing the milk, Sara absently stirred the liquid. She was not suffering from insomnia tonight due to an adrenaline rush, like the aftermath of the Search and Rescue mission. No, drat it, she had tossed and turned because of Gabe.

Following the absurd and sensual scenario she'd painted in her mind during her bubble bath, she'd hightailed it to her room and closed the door.

She'd heard the crackling of the flames in the fireplace, and longed to curl up in front of the hearth and stare into the fire until she was thoroughly relaxed.

But there was no way on earth that she was going into that living room where Gabe was sitting. She would have been too embarrassed to even look at the man. Not only that, but Gabe was very alert, had realized earlier that she was nervous. It was that sensitivity of his rising to the fore. She'd had no intention of being in the same room with him after the journey her wayward imagination had taken her on.

Once in bed after her bath, she'd been acutely aware of Gabe's presence in the house. He'd seemed to fill the small structure to overflowing, leaving her nowhere to escape from him.

Her senses seemed to be magnified as she heard lamps being turned off, his footsteps as he walked down the hall to the bathroom, then to the bedroom. The quiet click of his bedroom door had sounded as loud as a firecracker.

If only, *only,* she admonished herself, she'd been able to use the closing of that door as an ending, like in a movie. The credits would roll across her mental screen, then she'd have drifted off into delicious sleep.

But, oh, not Sara Ann Calhoun. She'd proceeded to imagine Gabe removing his clothes. Good Lord, she'd nearly died on the spot. Then he'd slipped naked...yep, naked as a jaybird...between the cool sheets. His dark hair and tanned skin had appeared scrumptious in her mind's eye against the pristine white of the soft pillow. Then...

"Shut up, shut up, Sara," she whispered. "You are out of your ever lovin' mind."

She was going crazy, she really was, and it was Gabriel Porter's fault. They would come cart her away to the funny farm, never to be heard from again.

So now, there she was, Sara mused, preparing hot milk in the hopes of dimming the image of Gabe enough to allow her to sleep.

The milk began to bubble and Sara turned off the stove. She grabbed a pot holder from the counter, lifted the pan from the burner and started to pour the milk into a mug she held in place with her free hand on the top of the stove.

"Sara?"

"Aaak!" she yelled, jerking in surprise at the sudden sound of Gabe's voice. The milk splashed over the back of the hand that held the mug. "Ow! Oh! Ow! I burned myself."

"Damn," Gabe said.

He crossed the room, and before Sara could react, had snatched the pan from her hand and put it on the counter. He gripped her wrist, spun her around and had cold water running over her injured hand as Sara managed to take her next breath.

"I'm sorry," he said. "I shouldn't have startled you like that. I heard a noise and thought I should investigate. Was the milk boiling?"

"No, no, it was just beginning to bubble," she said, attempting to pull her wrist free of his grasp.

"Leave it under the cold water for a while yet," he said.

"Yes, all right. It's not a bad burn though, because the milk wasn't hot enough to do much damage."

"Were you having trouble sleeping? Warm milk is usually a remedy for being unable to sleep."

"Really? Well, yes, I guess it is. I just happen to be fond of it for a snack."

"In the middle of the night?"

"Why not? That's plenty of cold water, don't you think?"

"No."

Sara turned her head toward him to argue the point, then forgot what she had been about to say.

Gabe was standing so close to her, she now realized, that he was mere inches away. He was wearing jeans with the snap undone, and his chest was bare. She was staring at the magnificence of his broad, nicely muscled chest, which was adorned with curly black hair. Beautiful.

She filled her senses with the sight of him, and his aroma of soap and wood smoke. If she leaned slightly forward, she could press her lips to the hard wall of his chest, then flick her tongue over the tanned skin to savor the taste.

Heat thrummed low within her, and her legs began to tremble.

"Sara," Gabe said, his voice gritty.

She shifted her gaze slowly to meet his, and her breath caught as she saw the stark desire radiating from the dark depths of his eyes.

"Sara," he repeated, then cleared his throat, "I think that's enough cold water on your hand. Let's get it dried off, then take a look at it."

Sara nodded, deciding not to trust her ability to speak. The pulsing heat within her had increased as she'd seen the evidence in Gabe's eyes of his want of her. He had said earlier that he was attracted to her, and that he wanted her was now definitely a given.

Dear heaven, she had to draw upon her own inner strength and resolve to be able to retain control of her raging emotional and physical reactions to Gabe.

If he had no interest in her whatsoever it might prickle her ego, but it would certainly remove him from the dangerous list. As things stood, she had an even more difficult situation to deal with because he was every bit aware of her as she was of him.

Gabe took the hand towel from the wood circle mounted on the wall, then slowly and gently began to pat the back of Sara's hand, cradling it in the palm of his free hand.

She watched the simple procedure, but as he drew the soft terry cloth down the length of each of her slender fingers in turn, the simple changed to sensuous, and her heart beat with a rapid tempo.

Her breasts grew heavy, achy, yearning for a soothing caress.

And the heat, the swirling heat, was consuming her in flames of passion.

"It's fine," Gabe said. "Your hand is fine."

"Yes." She looked up at him again. "Yes."

"But *I'm* not."

He dropped the towel into the sink, wove his fingers through her silky curls and lowered his head toward hers.

"Gabe, I..." she started.

But then all rational thought fled as he covered her lips with his.

Chapter Ten

She was definitely, Sara thought hazily, *sharing* this kiss with Gabriel Porter. And it was ecstasy and raging desire and heat pulsing low within her.

She slid her hands slowly up the broad expanse of Gabe's chest, tangling her fingertips through the dark, curly hair, savoring the feel of the hard muscles beneath, then finally encircling his neck with her hands.

Gabe dropped his hands from her hair to wrap his arms around her, drawing her closer to nestle against him. He delved his tongue into her mouth to meet her tongue in the sweet darkness. His arousal strained against the zipper on his jeans, and a groan rumbled in his chest.

Lord, how he wanted her. Wanted to make love with Sara Ann. Nothing, *nothing*, mattered but the two of them.

Gabe lifted his head a fraction of an inch to take a rough breath before attempting to speak.

"I want you, Sara," he said, his voice gritty with passion. "And you want me." He brushed his lips over hers. "I can feel you responding to me, giving of yourself. This is right, for both of us."

"Gabe..."

"Don't think, just feel," he went on. "This is *our* world, where we're stopping to smell the flowers."

Yes, Sara mused, their world, just the two of them, no one else, nothing else, except the flowers. They would stop and smell the beautiful flowers.

Stop....

The word suddenly echoed in Sara's mind, increasing in volume, beating against her brain.

She couldn't stop! she thought. She had to stay on track, working toward her goal, her purpose. To make love with Gabe was too risky, so very dangerous. Her attraction to him, her want of him, was so powerful it was a threat to her focus, her plan.

No, there wasn't room for pretty flowers, for stolen moments out of time, for making love with a man who caused her to experience physical and emotional reactions like none before.

Sara moved her hands to rest flat on Gabe's chest and pushed gently, delivering the message of wanting distance, wanting to be released from his embrace.

"No," she said.

Gabe dropped his arms to his sides, and Sara took a step backward. He looked directly into her eyes, a frown knitting his brows.

"Why?" he said. "Are you denying that you want to make love with me, Sara?"

She wrapped her hands around her elbows. "No, I can't deny it, but it isn't going to happen. You said it, Gabe. It would mean stopping, being pulled away from the path I'm traveling and have no intention of leaving. You, being with you... it's all too risky, too dangerous. Can you understand that?"

Gabe dragged a restless hand through his hair and nodded his head. "Oh, yeah, I understand what you're saying only too well. There was a time when I had tunnel vision about my career just as you have now. It's wrong, Sara. You're making a terrible mistake, and the price tag is enormous, more than you can even imagine. Don't do this to yourself. Hell, don't do this to *us*."

"There *is* no us," she said, her voice rising, "and there isn't going to be. I know where I'm going, and exactly what it will require to get there. I have to do it alone, Gabe. I don't intend to become involved with you, or any other man."

"Sara..."

"No more," she said, slicing one hand through the air. "I've admitted that I desire you, am very attracted to you. And, yes, we just *shared* that kiss. But I'm not going any further, Gabe, not one more inch.

Find someone else, someone who is willing to stop and smell the flowers you're talking about."

He didn't want anyone else, Gabe mentally yelled. Damn it, he wanted Sara Ann Calhoun.

"Good night, Gabe," she said. She turned and hurried from the room.

Gabe watched her go, his eyes narrowed in deep concentration.

No, he thought dryly, this wasn't a *good* night. His body was screaming for mercy, aching with heated arousal. Physically, he was a wreck. Emotionally? That was another story. *Confusion* was the word that applied, in spades.

He was determined to get through to Sara, to make her see that she was on a destructive course. He was doing that for *her*, hoping to keep her from having to pay the same piper he had.

Why? What did the emotions of possessiveness, protectiveness, really mean? He'd fallen in love many years before, and had married the woman who captured his heart.

But now he was a different man—changed, older and hopefully wiser. So, okay, it stood to reason that he might experience emotions that were foreign to him, to the man he'd become. The problem was, he just didn't know what they all meant!

"Lady," he said aloud, staring at the doorway Sara had gone through, "you are really getting to me. I want answers, Sara Ann, and I intend to get them."

In the morning, Sara postponed leaving her bedroom as long as possible, not wishing to encounter Gabe in the kitchen, nor wanting to have to sit across the table from him while they ate breakfast.

Having only enough time left for a quick cup of coffee, she squared her shoulders, smoothed the blouse of her uniform and marched down the hall, her chin lifted to a determined tilt.

She would be breezily pleasant, she decided, make some inane comment regarding the weather or the state of the economy, gulp down a mug of coffee, and exit stage left. Excellent plan.

"Good morning," she sang out as she zoomed into the kitchen. "I smell coffee. What a nice surprise to have it ready and waiting." She stopped and glanced around the room. "Well, for Pete's sake."

Gabe was not in the kitchen.

Crossing to the table, she read the note propped against the sugar bowl. Gabe had gone to the sheriff's office and would meet up with her there. It was signed with a sprawling *"G."*

A few minutes later, Sara sat down at the table with a mug of the hot coffee Gabe had prepared. She stared at the empty chair across from her, seeing Gabe as clearly in her mental vision as though he were actually sitting there. His words spoken in the tent on Thinker's Thumb echoed again in her mind.

Do you know the difference between being alone and being lonely?

Sara shivered as the silence in the room became suddenly oppressive.

Damn it, she fumed. She had no problem with being alone. She needed her freedom to be able to accomplish what she'd set out to do three years ago.

She'd dated while in Colorado, but had ended the relationship if the man she was seeing became too serious, wanted her to be a permanent part of his life. To make that type of commitment was to run the risk of having *her* goals diminished in importance.

Nothing was going to lure her from the path she'd chosen. She'd made that very clear to Gabe.

And she was not lonely.

But why did it seem so ominously quiet in that room? Why did it seem so empty?

"Forget it," she muttered, getting to her feet.

A short time later, she was speaking on the telephone to the nurse on duty at the hospital, inquiring about Jeb's condition.

The nurse cheerfully reported that Sheriff Broffy had spent a peaceful night, was crabby as an old bear this morning, and would be moved from intensive care to a private room after his sponge bath. Yes, certainly, Sara Ann could visit later, providing Martha Broffy hadn't strangled the patient in the meantime.

Sara laughed softly as she replaced the receiver, reaffirming in her mind the enchanting aura of closeness, of everyone-knows-everyone-else-and-isn't-that-nice that went along with living in a small town.

Yes, she mused, it was good to be home, back in Autumn where she belonged. It was warm and welcoming there, and the place where she would accomplish her goals. In her heart and soul, she would be able to say a proper and peaceful farewell to her father once she'd established a well-trained Search and Rescue team as a memorial to Patrick Calhoun.

When that was a fait accompli, she would...

Sara frowned and began to pace back and forth across the living room.

She would do what?

Halting in the middle of the room, she pressed one hand to her forehead and took a steadying breath.

Calm down, Sara. So, all right, she now realized that during the past three years she hadn't thought beyond obtaining the expertise she needed, returning to Autumn and establishing a top-notch Search and Rescue Unit to assure herself that never again would a life be lost because of an inadequate team.

Then? Well, she would provide ongoing training, fine-tuning her group, and continually seeking more men and women to join them.

There. That made sense. Between that program and her role of chief deputy—should she run for sheriff if Jeb retired?—she would be busy, busy, busy. Her workdays would be filled to overflowing with rewarding activities.

And her nights?

Do you know the difference between being alone and being lonely?

"Damn you, Gabriel," she said aloud, then stomped from the room.

At the sheriff's office, Sara greeted Dale Maddox, who was on the day shift, and inquired as to the whereabouts of Gabe. She needed him to sit down for a debriefing with regard to the Huxley mission so she could complete her report, she rattled on. Why she was explaining her reasons for looking for Gabe, she had no idea.

"He went to ticket an illegally parked vehicle that's taking up two spaces in front of Sissy's Bakery," Dale said. "Sissy's hopping mad. She said it's a hunter from Colorado, and the bozo—that's a direct quote—didn't even come into her shop to buy a doughnut."

"Shame on him," Sara said, smiling. "Anything else happening?"

"The drinkers are hung over and out on bail. I've called Yavapai County for court dates, and they'll get back to me. Don Harrison has called three times wanting to know who in the blue blazes is going to pay for his dairy cows those jokers shot. I told him it's up to the judge. Donny is not a happy farmer. That's all that's doin' so far, Sara Ann."

"Thank you," she said, nodding. "Would you ask Gabe to come into my office when he gets back?"

"Yep. I called over to Three C. I'm surely grateful that Jeb's going to be okay. If he retires, are you going to run for sheriff?"

"I'll think about that if the need arises," she said, starting toward her office.

"I'll bet you a bagel from Sissy's bakery that Jeb turns in his badge."

"We'll see."

In the office, Sara sat down behind her desk and stared at Jeb's empty chair across from her.

She was spending a lot of time staring at empty chairs this morning, she thought dryly.

Reaching for the top paper in her basket, she hesitated, looking at Jeb's desk again.

It was hard to imagine what it would be like not having Jeb Broffy as sheriff of Autumn. She had fond memories of stopping in at the office after school to tell him about her day. He had always kept hard candy in his right top desk drawer, a secret he said that belonged only to the two of them. On occasion when she was young, he would let her call Martha at home on the two-way radio, an event that made her feel terribly important and grown-up.

She sighed.

But time moved on, and so much was changing. So very, very much.

"Sara," Gabe said, striding into the room and bringing her from her reverie. "Dale said you wanted to see me." He stopped in front of her desk.

"Yes," she said, not looking at him. "Let's get the rescue mission report done, shall we? I've got such a pile of paperwork stacked up here, it's a crime, so I'd like to get that one out of the way. It shouldn't take too long because—"

"Sara..." he interrupted quietly.

She lifted her head slowly to meet his gaze, seeing the serious expression on his face.

"Yes?" she said.

"Good morning. I assume you discovered the coffee I made?"

"Yes, thank you, it was delicious. Now, about the report..."

"Whoa," he said, raising one hand. "Back up a minute."

"To what?"

"To the middle of last night. To what happened in the kitchen. To what you said about not being willing to stop and smell the flowers."

Sara glanced quickly at the open door, then glared up at Gabe.

"This is hardly the time or place for a personal discussion, Mr. Porter."

"Dale can't hear us. He said he was going into the back storeroom to get a box of Christmas decorations."

"Then try this," she said, narrowing her eyes. "The discussion in question is not going to take place at *any* time."

Gabe planted his hands flat on the desk and leaned toward her. She instinctively moved backward.

"Wrong," he said. "We're going to talk about it, Sara. We're going to discuss that, and a helluva lot of other things, too."

"I hope you enjoy chitchatting with yourself. It does take two to have a conversation."

He straightened and folded his arms loosely over his chest, a smile breaking across his face.

"And two to tango," he said. "And two, my sweet Sara Ann, to make love." He stroked his chin, a thoughtful expression replacing his grin. "You know, two could easily become my favorite number."

Chapter Eleven

Before Sara could think of an appropriate place to tell Gabriel Porter to put his ever-famous favorite number, Dale came into the office humming "Jingle Bells" and carrying a good-size, rather battered cardboard box.

"Oh, good grief," Sara said, "I recognize that box. Those are the same limp, faded Christmas decorations that have been used in this place since I was a kid."

"Yep," Dale said, setting the box on Jeb's desk. "There's never been any money in the budget for new stuff. Besides, we're all sentimentally attached to this junk." He pulled a plastic reindeer from the carton.

"Still missing one leg, I see. We never did figure out what happened to this guy's leg. It just disappeared."

"It gives him character," Gabe said, chuckling.

"Mmm," Sara said, frowning.

"Well, listen to you, Miss Scrooge," Gabe said. "It's less than two weeks until Christmas, and it sounds to me like you need an attitude adjustment before then. You're going to put up a Christmas tree at your house, aren't you?"

Sara shook her head. "No. The few ornaments my dad and I had were in a box stored at the antique shop. They were sold along with the inventory. Someone probably tossed them out. There's no point in putting up a tree and having to buy all new ornaments and lights. Besides, since my father won't be there to celebrate the holiday..." She shrugged.

"Well," Dale said, propping the three-legged reindeer against Jeb's wire basket, "Santa Claus comes to our house. When you have a three-year-old and a five-year-old, you go the whole nine yards. You know, leave cookies and milk out for Santa, that bit. I tried to convince my wife, Laura, that Santa would like a cold beer, but she wasn't buying the program."

Gabe chuckled, then crossed the room to peer into the box. He took out a stuffed Santa Claus sans beard.

"No beard?" he said, looking at Dale.

"Nope. It disappeared the same year as the reindeer's leg."

"Maybe we could glue some cotton onto his face," Gabe said.

"Yeah," Dale said, nodding. "I'll take it home and ask Laura to stick some cotton balls on the old guy."

Sara cleared her throat. "I hate to interrupt this executive session you two are having, but I'd like to get this rescue mission report done. Gabe, would you join me in the conference room, please?" She left the office with papers in one hand.

"The woman definitely has an attitude problem about Christmas," Gabe said.

"Well, it was rough on her losing her daddy like she did," Dale said. "I imagine the holidays are still difficult for Sara Ann to get through. You'd better get in that conference room, Gabe, before she starts spitting nails."

"Yep."

The report was finished in record time, and Sara told Gabe that he had a remarkable memory for details.

"Comes from being an attorney once upon a time," he said.

Dale poked his head into the room. "Got a call. Tip Hudson has three hunters held at gunpoint in his kitchen. He caught them trespassing on his property, and didn't take kindly to the fact."

"I'll go," Sara said, getting to her feet. "The door is unlocked at the house, Gabe. I'm going over to Three C after work to see Jeb. I'll catch up with you at the house tonight if we don't happen to meet back here."

"Fine," he said, watching her hurry from the room.

* * *

The afternoon was busy. Sara brought in Tip's captured and very shaken up hunters, learned that Randy and Gabe were out on separate calls, then went back out herself to rescue a treed hunter that Tony Turner was threatening to shoot with buckshot for cutting through a section of Tony's fence.

It was close to seven o'clock when Sara stepped out of the elevator on the third floor of the Three C hospital and headed for Jeb's room.

The sheriff was propped up in bed against a stack of pillows, his nose buried in a gun magazine. Martha sat in a chair next to the bed, busily knitting with bright red and green yarn.

"Is this where the party is?" Sara said, smiling as she came into the room. She went to the bed and kissed Jeb on the cheek. "Hello, Troublemaker. It's amazing what some people will do to get attention."

"Isn't it though?" Martha said, her fast, busy fingers continuing to knit.

Sara pulled a chair next to the bed on the opposite side from Martha.

"You look wonderful, Jeb," Sara said.

"I'm fine, Sara Ann," he said, patting her hand. "Tell me what's happening at the office."

"Jeb Broffy," Martha said, a warning tone to her voice.

"Hell's fire, Martha," he said, "I'm going to retire, I've promised you that, but I can still check up on my town and county, you know."

"You're really going to retire?" Sara said, frowning.

"Yes, it's time," he said. "You'll be acting sheriff until the election in the spring, Sara Ann. I hope I don't die of boredom."

"You won't," Martha said. "First order of business is our cruise, just as soon as Doc Hartman says you're fit to go."

"Do you think you'll run for sheriff, Sara Ann?" Jeb said. "You could handle the job very well, my girl."

"Thanks for the vote of confidence," she said. "I have plenty of time to decide. My first priority is establishing and training a Search and Rescue team."

"They don't come much better than Gabe's Back Country Unit," Jeb said.

"They belong to Copper County. I want my own team in Canyon County."

"Why couldn't you and Gabe work together?" Martha said.

"No, I don't think so," Sara said.

"Don't be so quick to dismiss the idea, miss," Jeb said. "You've only got so many hours in a given day. If you joined up with Gabe you'd have time for other things in your life besides work."

"Which might mean," Doc Hartman said, coming into the room, "that you might eat decent, Sara Ann, and not look like a toothpick. Martha, Sara Ann, go home. It's lights-out time for Jeb."

"Hell's fire," Jeb said.

The trio left the room.

In the hallway, Doc Hartman said he wanted to speak to Sara Ann for a moment. Martha bid them good-night, and Sara followed the doctor to a small office at the end of the hall, curious as to what he had on his mind.

In the room, Doc Hartman shut the door, then waved Sara onto a chair. He pulled another one close to her and sat down.

"We have to talk, Sara Ann," he said, no hint of a smile on his face. "I reached a decision three years ago, and Jeb went along with it. Now, I'm beginning to believe I made a mistake."

"What are you talking about?"

"Jeb and I were playing gin rummy this afternoon, and he was speaking of you. He's worried because you're determined to train a Search and Rescue Unit here, to make certain that nothing happens again like it did to your daddy."

"That's right."

"It's a fine, noble idea, Sara Ann, except Jeb feels you're nearly obsessed with that goal. *That*, Sara Ann, is *not* good."

"It's the kind of dedication it will take, Doc," she said, her voice rising. "I owe it to my father. It's a memorial of sorts to him."

"Sara Ann, listen to me," the doctor said gently. "No one could have saved Patrick Calhoun. The finest Back Country Unit in the state could have been called in, and the outcome would have been the same.

Since the group that *did* go was disbanded, I decided to let you place the blame there. But now? Sweet girl, you've narrowed your life down to a pinpoint because of something you *believe* to be true but isn't."

"What are you saying?" she whispered, feeling the color drain from her face.

"Honey, Patrick was drunk, was celebrating heaven only knows what. He didn't even have a jacket on, just a flannel shirt. The mission report had the facts, but there was no need in my mind at the time to tell you that Patrick was responsible for his own death."

"No," she said, shaking her head. "No, that's not true. It can't be true."

Doc Hartman took both of her hands in his and looked directly into her green eyes, which were now brimming with tears.

"It is true," he said. "I'm sorry, Sara Ann. I did what I thought was best, and Jeb agreed. We didn't falsify records, the team was disbanded anyway, so why force you to deal with Patrick's irresponsibility, as well as his death? Thing is, you're hell-bent on a quest that isn't based on the truth.

"I'm not saying that putting together a first-rate Search and Rescue Unit is wrong, Sara Ann, but you need to weigh and measure all the facts as they truly are. You need to reevaluate your priorities, get some balance in your life. *No one could have saved Patrick Calhoun's life.*"

"Dear God," Sara said, pulling her hands free. "I can't believe this. I . . ." Tears spilled onto her cheeks.

"I wanted... needed... to set things to rights for my father. That's all I've thought about since he died and—" She pressed her fingertips to her lips to stifle a sob threatening to escape.

"I'm sorry, Sara Ann," Doc Hartman said, sounding very weary. "Jeb and I did what we did out of love for you, but that doesn't erase the fact that we were wrong. I hope you can find it in your heart to forgive us. But even more important is that you step back, take a hard look at your life, and see what you're doing to yourself."

Sara stumbled to her feet, dashing the tears from her cheeks.

"I have to go," she said, her voice quivering. "I need to be alone, to think, to... Oh, God, I don't know where to put this."

"Honey, don't drive back to Autumn yet. Wait until you've calmed down a bit."

"No, no, I must go. I don't have hard feelings toward you and Jeb, Doc. I don't, I promise. It's just so much for me to digest. My world is suddenly turned upside down. I'm confused. I feel so lost. I..." She patted him absently on the shoulder with a trembling hand. "I have... to go home... now, Doc. I... Yes, I need... to be alone." She hurried from the room, nearly running.

Doc turned to watch her go, concern etched on his wrinkled face.

"I'm sorry, Sara Ann," he said softly, tears misting his own eyes. "I'm mighty sorry, sweet girl."

Sara hardly remembered driving from the hospital to Autumn. She was shaken to the very core of her being, Doc Hartman's words beating unmercifully against her mind.

It was as though she'd been flung into a dark abyss, she thought frantically, with nothing to hold on to, no anchor to keep her solidly in one place. The bottom had fallen out of her world.

She tried desperately, and failed, to cling to the fact that establishing and training a superb Back Country Search and Rescue Unit was an admirable goal under *any* circumstances. While a small part of her knew that was very true, it was overshadowed by the realization that *her* raison d'être for the past three years had been ripped away, totally destroyed.

All the hard work, the long hours of studying and training, the return to Autumn, had all been focused on her father, her memorial to him, tangible evidence that while she couldn't bring him back to her, she could at least assure the safety of others in the future.

Lord, what a joke. A cruel joke. It was a sham, her great goal she'd been determined to achieve. Yes, the unit would benefit others, but it would have nothing to do with emotionally righting the wrong done to her father.

Patrick Calhoun had behaved as he had a multitude of times while she was growing up, acting without one rational thought of what the consequences might be. He'd paid a heavy price for his immaturity on that occasion: he'd died.

Doc Hartman's revelations did not, Sara knew, tarnish the memory of her father in her heart, soul and mind. Patrick was Patrick. What the truth *had* done was to cause her to now view her life as a tangled maze of confusion and self-doubt.

If she removed the equation of her father's death from her purpose, her goals, what did *she* want, really want?

Dear heaven, she didn't know.

More by rote than actual awareness of what she was doing, she turned into the driveway at her house, then pressed the button to open the garage door.

Only when she'd entered the house to find lamps softly glowing in the living room and a fire crackling in the hearth, did she remember that Gabe's vehicle had been outside and he was there in her home.

Her breath caught as she stared across the living room. Gabe was dozing, had not stirred when she'd come in.

And Gabriel Porter was sitting in Patrick Calhoun's special chair.

Chapter Twelve

The amalgam of emotions churning within Sara spun tighter and tighter, creating a dark funnel that consumed her like a twisting, turning tornado.

The multitude of issues she was suddenly attempting to deal with in her unsettled life blended together to focus on one entity—Gabe.

Whether or not the fury building within her was reasonable or rational, she didn't even stop to consider. She was emotionally overloaded, simply had far too much to deal with, and there was now a target for her exhausted state of mind.

She flung her gloves, jacket and hat onto the sofa and stomped across the room to stand towering over a sleeping Gabe, where he was slouched in her father's chair. Her hands curled into fists and came to rest firmly on her hips.

"Gabriel Porter," she yelled, "get your worthless carcass out of that chair!"

Gabe jerked awake, blinked in confusion, then stared up at Sara.

"What?" he said. He shook his head slightly to dispel the last of the fogginess of sleep.

"You heard me," she said, not lowering the volume of her voice. Unnoticed tears spilled onto her cheeks. "No one—*no one*—sits in that chair. It belonged to my father. It's his. Damn you, Gabe, it's his."

Gabe's dark brows knitted in a frown and he narrowed his eyes as he looked at Sara intently.

Something was very wrong here, he mused. Sara was crying, her face was ghostly pale, and there were purple smudges beneath her emerald eyes. There was a fragile aura surrounding her, as though she might shatter into a million pieces at any given moment, and her voice was trembling. There was far more going on than his having sat in Patrick Calhoun's chair.

He got slowly to his feet, his intense gaze never leaving hers.

"I'm sorry, Sara," he said quietly. "I had no idea you didn't want anyone to use this chair. My mistake. It won't happen again."

It was too much, it really was. The soft, soothing caress of Gabe's voice flowed over Sara, draining her of her last ounce of energy.

She could have handled it, she thought frantically, if he'd hollered right back at her, providing fuel for her anger. But this... this damnable sensitivity of his was going to be her undoing.

"Oh, damn you," she said, then sank her face into her hands and gave way to her tears.

Gabe's frown deepened, he hesitated a moment, then stepped closer to her to wrap his arms around her. She grabbed handfuls of his shirt, buried her face in his chest and wept.

And Gabe held her. He moved one hand to rest lightly on the back of her head, dipping his fingertips into her silky curls. His other arm encircled her back, holding her fast, nestled to his body.

Sara cried as though her heart were breaking, and Gabe clenched his jaw, forcing himself not to speak.

Voices in his mind demanded to know the cause of her upset, the source of her sorrow. Where were the dragons hiding that he would slay for her at any cost? He would set to rights, by damn, whatever was wrong. He would dry her tears, protect her, keep her safe, stand between her and whatever or whoever had caused her to cry.

Sara drew a breath that ended in a wobbly sob, then lifted her head slowly to look up at Gabe. He smiled at her warmly, gently, which nearly caused her to burst into tears again.

As she began to ease out of his embrace, he tightened his hold, refusing to release her. With one arm still firmly across her back, he reached into his back pocket and produced a pristine white handkerchief.

"Thank you," she mumbled, then dabbed at her nose. "I...I apologize for my behavior. You couldn't possibly have known that I'm sentimentally attached to that chair." She paused. "*I* don't even sit in it, which, now that I think about it, is silly. It's a comfortable old chair, and should be used, not kept as a shrine or something. Feel free to use it, Gabe."

"Fine. That covers that subject. Now would you like to talk about what's *really* upsetting you?"

"The chair. I just wasn't prepared to see you sitting in my father's chair."

"That might have been the last straw, but you've been out collecting a helluva lot of other straws. You went to see Jeb. Is he all right?"

"Yes, yes, he's doing very well. He's resigning his position of sheriff as of tomorrow. Gabe, would you please let me go?"

"No."

"Look, I appreciate your patience. I didn't behave well when I came in here. I've had a difficult day, that's all. I'll just toddle off to bed and be as good as new in the morning. Okay?"

"No."

"Damn it, Gabriel—"

"Talk to me, Sara," he interrupted. "You're hiding behind those walls of yours again. I'm here, I care, I want to know what upset you. Trust me, will you?

You're so damn determined to do everything alone, and it doesn't have to be that way."

"Yes, it does," she said, shoving against his chest.

He released her and she backed up, forgetting the sofa was behind her. She sat down on it with a thud when the cushion hit the back of her knees.

Gabe moved quickly to sit next to her, sliding one arm across her shoulders.

"Why?" he said. "Why does it have to be that way? I'm not a threat to you, Sara. Granted, I think your tunnel vision regarding your career is a mistake, a grave error on your part, but even if I talk until I'm blue in the face, you're the only one who can really change the course you're on."

"Wrong," she said, fresh tears filling her eyes. "My life has been changed by other people, not by me. My goals, my purpose..." She threw up her hands. "I just don't know what to do, or think."

"About what?"

"Everything," she said, her voice gaining volume again. "I knew who I was, where I was going, and why. Now? It's all a confusing jumble. I wanted to have the best Search and Rescue Unit in the state, the very best one as a memorial to my father but..."

"But?" he prompted.

"Even if I'd *had* that unit assembled, it wouldn't have made a difference on the day my father died. I couldn't have saved him, no one could. He wasn't wearing a jacket, Gabe." Two tears slid down her cheeks. "No jacket. Isn't that something? Doc Hartman told me tonight at Three C. No jacket."

"Lord," Gabe said, his eyes riveted on her face.

"I'm confused. I'm tired," she said, her voice shaking. "I can't remember right now if *I* wanted to set up a Search and Rescue Unit, or if it was all for my father. I just don't know. If it was for Patrick Calhoun, then what I'm doing doesn't make sense. It's so risky to love people, because you never know what they might do. Can't you see that?"

"Sara..."

"And then there's you," she rambled on, poking him in the chest with one finger.

"Me?" he said, raising one eyebrow.

"Yes. You've caused me nothing but grief since you came into my life. Your Search and Rescue Unit was supposed to be inadequate because you're volunteers, but you're excellent, damn it. Even Moses is far better than most, and he should be strolling around golf courses or something, not climbing mountains. Then when you kiss me, I melt, just dissolve into a ridiculous puddle, and I really am angry at you about that."

A slow smile began to creep onto Gabe's face.

"But did you stop there? Oh, no, not Gabriel Porter," she said. "You just had to ask me that question, didn't you? Do you know the difference between being alone and being lonely, Sara Ann? Ohh, I could strangle you for that, I really could."

Gabe's smile grew bigger.

"Don't you dare smile," she shrieked. "No! When you touch me, kiss me, hold me, when you *smile*, I... Oh, dear God, Gabe, my father didn't even have on a warm jacket."

"Ah, Sara," he said, his smile instantly replaced by an expression of concern.

He slid one arm beneath her knees, shifted the one from her shoulders to her back, and lifted her onto his lap. Slipping both arms around her, he held her close. She rested her head on his shoulder and fought against the tears that threatened to consume her again.

"Cry some more if you want to," Gabe said quietly. "Lord knows you have the right. You have a lot on your plate to deal with."

"Crying doesn't solve a thing, not a thing. Oh, Gabe, I feel as though I'm floundering in a foreign sea. I don't know who I am right now, what I want, where I'm going. I've got to start from scratch, sift and sort everything, figure out where I belong. But I'm tired, so very tired."

"You can start thinking about it tomorrow. Just relax now. Listen to the fire in the hearth. Can you feel it? It's warm, soothing. Everything's going to fine, Sara, just fine."

She sighed and snuggled closer to him, allowing the power of his body, the strength of his arms, to wrap her in a protective cocoon where she didn't have to do anything but be.

Gabe felt so wonderful and smelled so good. He was holding her as though she were a child, but she was very aware that she was a woman, and he was most definitely a man. His thighs were rock hard, taut and muscled, an enticing contrast to the soft curve of her bottom.

Oh, yes, she could feel the warmth from the fire in the hearth, but there was also heat emanating from Gabe's massive body that was causing a thrumming heat deep and low within her.

She wanted him, wanted to make love with him. This time she *would* stop and smell the flowers, the beautiful flowers. She couldn't deal with her reality right now, because it was just too much to handle all at once. Tomorrow she would think about it, just as Gabe had said. But now?

She lifted her head. "Gabe?"

He met her gaze, nearly groaning aloud as he saw the smoky hue of desire in her emerald eyes. She felt like heaven in his arms, was nestled perfectly against him as though she'd been custom-made just for him. His arousal was a heavy, aching, coiling tension building with every beat of his racing heart.

His lips captured hers in a kiss that was rough, urgent, hungry with want and need. His tongue plummeted into her mouth, finding her tongue, dancing, dueling, heightening his passion even more.

Sara returned the kiss in total abandon, savoring his taste, inhaling his aroma of fresh air, soap and man, feeling his manhood pressing against her, hearing the moan that rumbled in his chest.

Gabe drew a ragged breath, then his mouth melted over hers once more, gentle now, seductive, sensuous in its softness. His hands roamed restless across her back, one moving to cup a breast, bringing a sigh of pure pleasure whispering from Sara's throat.

He pulled the blouse of her uniform free, then deftly unbuttoned it, his lips never leaving hers. He stroked one breast with a work-roughened thumb, the nipple becoming a taut bud beneath the filmy lace of her bra.

Sara whimpered, arching her back to press her breast closer to his hand, seeking the soothing caress he alone could provide.

The only sounds in the room were their quickening breaths and the crackling flames of the fire.

In a smooth motion, Gabe got to his feet, laid Sara on the sofa, then stretched out next to her, resting on his forearm. He spread open her blouse, his heated gaze sweeping over her lace-covered breasts, and the dewy skin exposed above her belt.

He looked into her eyes again, feeling like a drowning man being pulled further and further into their beckoning green depths.

He kissed her again, his hand caressing first one breast, the other, then skimming down her slender thigh and over to the heat of her femininity hidden beneath the khaki slacks.

"Oh, Sara," he said, close to her lips. His voice was gritty with passion, and a pulse beat wildly in his temple. "I want you so damn much. I ache for you, Sara Ann."

"I want you, too, Gabe," she whispered. "You said I shouldn't think about anything until tomorrow, and you're right. All that matters is now. We'll stop and smell the flowers, just the way you've been telling me about. Tonight is ours. Make love with me, Gabe, please."

His mouth came down hard onto hers in a searing kiss, and he could feel the last of his control slipping beyond his reach. It seemed as though an eternity had passed as he'd waited for this moment when he would mesh his body with Sara's, take them both to a world that would belong only to them.

But...

Niggling little voices began to hum in his mind, gaining strength and volume, their message becoming starkly clear. Sara's words were echoing over and over.

I don't know who I am right now, what I want, where I'm going.

Gabe tore his mouth from hers, and mustered his last ounce of willpower.

"No. Sara, no."

She blinked hazily, trying to comprehend what he was saying.

"Gabe?"

He rolled off the sofa to his feet, and dragged both hands down his face before looking at her again.

"Cover yourself," he said, frowning.

She gripped the edges of the blouse with both hands and struggled to an upright position.

"Gabe?" she repeated.

"Damn it, Sara," he said, none too quietly. "It's no good, not like this."

"I don't understand," she said, forcing strength into her voice.

Gabe turned and went to the fireplace. He gripped the edge of the mantel, then stared down into the leaping flames, his back to Sara.

With trembling fingers, she quickly buttoned her blouse, her heart racing as she waited for Gabe to explain the reason for the abrupt halt to their lovemaking.

Why? her mind hammered. Was he rejecting her? Had he suddenly realized that he just didn't want her, didn't want to make love with her? Dear heaven, the mere fleeting thought of that being true hurt so badly, caused a pain like nothing she'd experienced before in a place within her she hadn't known existed.

Gabe shifted to face her again, shoving his hands into the back pockets of his jeans.

"You know I want you, Sara," he said, his voice very low. "I want to make love with you more than I have ever wanted anyone."

"Then why..."

"Just listen, okay? I kept hearing what you said about not knowing who you are, what you want, where you're going. Tonight you're in limbo, waiting for a fresh day so you can start tackling the confusion in your life."

Sara nodded. "Yes, I'm stopping tonight to smell the flowers."

"No, you're not. That's the point. When we make love, Sara, it has to be a part of the lives we're living. I realize now how important that is. You said you had no room for me, for us, because you had a master plan, a course of action all worked out."

"But..."

"Tonight?" he went on. "You've had the rug pulled out from under you. Sara, if we made love now, in the emotional place where you are, it would simply be something to fill a void at a time when you've postponed what you have to deal with. It's wise to put it all on the shelf until you've had a good night's sleep. What we would have shared is too important to be taken lightly. It should be reality, Sara, and you're not dealing in reality tonight."

"But the flowers," she said, lunging to her feet. "What about the damnable flowers you keep harping about?"

"The flowers don't mean a tinker's damn if you haven't learned to fit them into your day-to-day life. This—" he swept one arm toward the sofa "—was by default, along with the flowers, because you've stepped away, done a time-out from your problems. Well, damn it, Sara Calhoun, that's not good enough."

"Well, excuse me all to hell and back, Gabriel Porter. I didn't realize that you were running this show with the only voice allowed to be heard. You're acting like a spoiled brat."

"No," he said, his voice suddenly quiet again. "I'm a man who respects himself and you. We both deserve better than what this night would have been."

Sara pressed her fingertips to her now throbbing temples.

"I don't believe this," she said. "You're talking in riddles, not making any sense. Fine. Dandy. Whatever. You've just frosted the crummy cake this day has been. I've had enough of this day, and, Lord knows, I've had enough of your mumbo jumbo. Good night."

She spun around and left the room.

"Porter," Gabe said aloud, his gaze flickering over the sofa where he'd been with Sara, "you're either a noble son of a gun, or you're certifiably insane."

Chapter Thirteen

During the next three days, Sara had the strange sensation of being rather removed from herself, as though she were standing outside of her body as an observer watching a movie. Everything she did had a foreign feeling to it as she tried desperately to determine how she now viewed her career, her goals.

The same questions plagued her during her waking hours and on into her dreams at night. Was she content as a law enforcement officer? Did she still have the drive, the tunnel vision she'd had regarding establishing a superior Search and Rescue Back Country Unit? Was what she wanted changed since removing the memorial to her father from the equation?

The questions hammered at her, but the answers remained elusive.

She saw little of Gabe, as everyone in the sheriff's department was busy, responding to call after call. She and Gabe were in and out of the house and office at different hours, and did nothing more than acknowledge each other in passing.

In addition to dealing with the turmoil in her mind regarding her career, there was nowhere to hide, she knew, from the mental image of Gabe that hovered constantly in her mind's eye. The details of the night when she'd arrived home to find him sleeping in her father's chair were etched indelibly in her memory.

To her dismay, the remembrance of Gabe's kiss and touch had caused a flush to stain her cheeks, her breasts to become heavy and achy, and desire to thrum hot and low within her.

She would envision his smile... dear heaven, that smile... remember the ecstasy of his hand cupping her breast, actually smell his unique aroma, and hear the deep, velvet-soft timbre of his voice.

What did it all mean? she wondered. Why was Gabe capable of capturing her mind and memory? What were all these new emotions that tumbled one into the next? How was it possible that Gabe had awakened a depth of womanly desire within her that she, herself, had not even known she possessed?

But those questions, as well, went unanswered.

On the evening of the third day since the night of the "Patrick's Chair" incident, as Sara now referred to it in her befuddled mind, she arrived home just before seven o'clock. The day had been fairly quiet as more and more hunters left Autumn and the melting snow removed the hazard from the roads.

She'd visited a grumpy Jeb and a smiling Martha at Three C, checked in once more with the deputy on duty at the office, then headed for home.

She hesitated before entering the house, having seen Gabe's vehicle out front and the glow of light behind the closed drapes.

Hold it, ma'am, she told herself, one hand on the doorknob. She had to get in touch with her inner voice and decide if she was excited over the prospect of an evening shared with Gabe, or filled with dread. Surely she knew the answer to *something*.

She stood statue still, waiting for the message she sought. With an unladylike snort of disgust, she realized that the only missive reaching her brain was the fact that her toes were freezing. After rolling her eyes heavenward, she opened the door, went into the living room and shoved the door closed behind her.

Her step faltered and she stopped in her tracks as she viewed the scene before her, unaware that her eyes were widened and her mouth had dropped open.

Across the room, Gabriel Porter was busily decorating a Christmas tree.

"Hi," he said, glancing at her with a smile. He redirected his attention to the string of multicolored lights he was placing on the tree. "I'm glad you're home at a decent hour. I wouldn't have wanted you to miss out on all the fun."

Sara snapped her mouth closed as she finally realized it was open, then walked slowly forward as she removed her jacket and hat and dropped them onto the sofa.

"What..." she started, then quit talking as she heard the strange squeak that was supposed to be her voice. She cleared her throat and tried again. "What do you think you're doing?"

Gabe turned to look at her, frowning slightly. "You don't know? You're in worse shape than I thought, Miss Scrooge. This is a Christmas tree, I'm decorating it, and Santa Claus is coming in a few days."

"I know what it is," she said, hurrying to stand in front of him. "I meant, what are you doing with it in my living room?"

"Like I said, I'm decorating it. You're just in time to help."

"Don't play dumb, Gabriel. I distinctly recall saying that I didn't plan to put up a Christmas tree because I don't have any decorations and since my father... well, I don't have any decorations."

"No problem. I have lots of decorations. As for the tree, I grew it myself. I went over to Rio this afternoon to check on things at my ranch after I visited Jeb. It was a good thing I did, because my trees have been selling like hotcakes. I have a terrific crew at my place. Anyway, I snatched this beauty up. I'm a helluva Christmas tree grower, don't you think?"

Sara looked at the tree.

It was big and beautiful, and so perfectly shaped that it was hard to believe that it was real and not artificial. There had never been a tree this lovely in the house, as the budget had always dictated that Patrick buy the scraggly left-in-the-corner tree that no one wanted.

"Yes," she said, smiling slightly, "it's very nice. It must give you a tremendous sense of accomplishment to know you grew it yourself. It's just that, well, I thought it might be easier emotionally if I didn't put up a tree because my father wouldn't be here to share it."

"Sara," Gabe said quietly, "do you really think Patrick Calhoun would have wanted you to not celebrate the holidays? I never met him, but from what I've heard about him, I believe he'd fully expect you to have moved forward in your life after he was gone."

"Yes," she said with a sigh. "I suppose he would want me to do that. Actually, I was until... never mind. Look, let's compromise. You go ahead and decorate the tree, and I'll busy myself doing something else. I certainly thank you for bringing such a gorgeous one from your ranch, but I just don't have the proper holiday spirit to get all charged up over decorating it."

"All right," he said, nodding slowly, "I'll trim it." He paused. "Think about this, though, Sara. We've been working very hard the past few days, reality to the max. So, this is legitimate time out to literally smell the flowers, or in this case, the pine tree." He took a deep breath. "That is fantastic."

Sara matched his deep breath. "Yes, it does smell good." But she hadn't been moving in a world of reality the past three days. She'd been stumbling around in a fog of confusion. "It has a delightful fragrance."

"Well, stopping to smell the flowers is more than just sniffing the air, you know. It's an attitude. Are you certain you won't help me trim this beauty?"

"No. No, thank you. I'm going to have a sandwich. Are you hungry?"

"No, I had a hamburger before I came here."

"Fine."

Sara turned and hurried from the room.

Gabe watched her go, aware of the frustration he was feeling.

Sara was definitely back to business as usual. Work, work, work, with little time for anything or... damn it, *anyone* else. He'd been so positive that the Christmas tree would lighten her up, get her into the holiday spirit.

During the last few years of his marriage, his wife had hired an outfit to come in and assemble and decorate an artificial tree. He'd leave for work in the morning, then come home that night and there it would be in all its phony glory. Ridiculous. And very, *very* wrong.

He looked at the doorway Sara had gone through, a deep frown on his face.

What was happening right now in this house, he thought, shaking his head in disgust, was nearly as bad as those crummy trees he'd found in his living room in Los Angeles.

Sara was a disinterested sideline observer of the trimming of the tree. He had been thoroughly enjoying decorating the tree, but an edge had been taken from the pleasure, because he'd wanted to share the event with Sara.

Interesting, he thought. Sara Ann Calhoun was definitely becoming a major player in his life, a very important person.

Gabe finished placing the lights on the branches, then unplugged them before starting to hang the ornaments. He worked steadily but was aware that he was waiting, hoping, that Sara would return to the living room.

Over a half an hour later, Sara reappeared carrying a tray, which she set on the coffee table.

"I made hot chocolate," she said. "Would you like some?"

"Hey, perfect," he said, turning to smile at her. He held a gold foil star in one hand. "The tree is finished, except for this." He bowed, then extended the star toward Sara. "Ma'am, you may have the honor of putting this in place. It's the finishing touch, the big finale."

Gabe was trying so hard, Sara thought. It had been a sweet gesture to bring over the tree from his ranch and tote in the boxes of ornaments. It wasn't his fault that she couldn't muster up any enthusiasm, any holiday spirit. But the least she could do was be polite, put forth a bit of effort to acknowledge his sensitivity. Oh, yes, there was that Gabriel Porter sensitivity again.

"Sara?"

"I accept the honor you're bestowing upon me, sir," she said, forcing a lightness to her voice. She took the star, then looked up at the top of the tall tree. "I'll get a chair."

"No need." He stepped behind her, gripped her waist and lifted her off the floor.

"Gabe," she gasped. "For heaven's sake, put me down."

He chuckled and hoisted her higher. "It's all part of the service, ma'am. Set the star on the very top."

Sara laughed and grasped the top branch, slipping the star into place.

Gabe was lifting her as though she weighed no more than a feather pillow, she realized. His hands were firm, so very strong, and the heat from where he was holding her was spiraling through her.

"There," she said. "I did it."

He set her back on her feet. "Now, humor me, Sara. Stand right there. Don't move." He hurried to turn off the lamps, the leaping flames in the fireplace the only remaining luminescence. "Ready? I'm going to plug in the tree lights."

"Go for it," she said, clasping her hands loosely in front of her.

He inserted the plug into the wall socket.

Sara's breath caught as the tree came alive in a spectacle of beauty, a magnificent rainbow. The ornaments that had simply been there were suddenly mirrors of a multitude of colors, casting a wondrous glow over the room.

"Oh, Gabe," she whispered, "it's beautiful. I've never seen such a wonderful Christmas tree."

He walked slowly toward her. "*You're* beautiful," he said, a husky quality to his voice. "The colors are pouring over you like a rainbow waterfall."

She glanced down at herself, then smiled as she met his gaze when he stopped in front of her.

"Now *you're* in the rainbow waterfall," she said. "Thank you, Gabe, for the tree. I wasn't gracious about it at all, and I apologize. It's so lovely."

He cradled her face in his hands. "You're welcome." He dipped his head and brushed his lips over hers. "I'm very glad you like the tree, Sara."

She opened her mouth slightly to reply, but before she could speak, Gabe captured her lips with his, his tongue slipping seductively into her mouth.

Her arms floated upward to encircle his neck, and she met his tongue eagerly with her own. He dropped his hands from her face to wrap his arms around her, nestling her to him. His arousal was instantaneous, pressing heavily against her.

Rainbows, Sara thought dreamily, and flowers. Christmas trees and beautifully colored waterfalls. The scent of pine, the feel of Gabe. Ecstasy.

The kiss deepened and passions soared.

Without breaking the kiss, Gabe lowered Sara to the floor, and she went willingly. He stretched out next to her, half-covering her body with his own.

"Sara," he said, raising his head a fraction of an inch and looking directly into her eyes.

That's all he said, just her name, yet she knew what he was asking. And just as clearly, with a sense of rightness and immeasurable joy, she gave her answer.

"Yes."

Slowly and with infinite care, he removed her clothing, paying homage with his lips to her exquisite body as it was revealed to him. The rainbow waterfall created a glowing, ethereal aura around them, enclosing them in a wondrous world that was theirs alone.

When Gabe stood to shed his own clothes, Sara instantly missed his touch, heat, the every essence of him. The caresses he had placed on her dewy skin, she returned with her eyes, desire radiating from the smoky green depths.

Oh, dear heaven, she thought, he was so beautiful. He was towering above her boldly nude, his manhood a vivid declaration of his want of her. Each section of his magnificent body was perfectly proportioned to the next. His power was visible, her anticipation of what he would bring to her causing a pulsing rhythm low within her.

The rainbow waterfall did nothing to diminish his masculinity. Rather it enhanced it, making him appear like a gladiator from another world, who had stepped out of time and an unknown place to become her lover.

Sara lifted her arms to welcome Gabe back into her embrace.

Sara, Gabe's mind hummed, as he stretched out next to her again. *Sara Ann.*

He kissed her deeply, then shifted to one breast, drawing the lush bounty into his mouth, flickering his tongue over the nipple that became a taut button. Resting his weight on one forearm, he splayed his hand on her flat stomach, then lower, and lower yet.

He wanted her, his mind thundered. Yet, he didn't wish to rush this moment, what they would ultimately share. The feathery sensation of Sara's fingertips skimming over his back was erotic in its gentleness, like a tiny butterfly tantalizing with the fluttering motion of its gossamer wings.

Sara was so beautiful, so delicate, like a china doll that must be treated with infinite care so as not to be crushed. Never before had he been so aware of his own size and strength, of the power of his masculinity.

Gabe moved to Sara's other breast, laving the nipple with his tongue, glorying in the purrs of pleasure murmuring from her lips. To please her was foremost in his mind. She was giving of herself so willingly, honestly, and he cherished that realization as being a very precious, treasured gift.

How very, *very* important Sara had become to him, he thought hazily.

He wanted to protect her, care for her, keep her from harm's way.

He wanted to hear her wind chime laughter and see smiles that reached her eyes and caused them to sparkle like emeralds.

He wanted to tear down her walls, brick by emotional brick, prove to her that being with him would not bring her heartache or pain, that it was a risk she could run with no heavy price tag to pay.

As he captured her mouth again, a question flickered across his passion-laden mind, then settled firmly into place, not to be ignored. *Was he falling in love with Sara Ann Calhoun?*

He raised his head to look into her eyes, to see if, somehow, the answer to the question would be *there*, waiting for him. But he saw only desire, the smoky hue of Sara's green eyes, the message of need and want that heightened his passion even more.

"Please, Gabe," Sara whispered. "I want you. I need you...now."

"Yes."

He shifted over her, catching his weight on his forearms, then entered her, closing his eyes for a moment to savor the ecstasy of meshing his body with hers. He filled her, and she received all that he brought to her.

"Ah, Sara," he said, his voice gritty.

As he began to move, she matched his rhythm in perfect synchronization, as though the ancient dance had been created just for them. A soft smile touched her lips as she wrapped her arms around his strong, glistening back.

Harder. Faster. The tensions built within them with a sweet, coiling pain, bringing them closer and closer to the end of the glorious journey.

"Gabe!" Sara called, her hold on him tightening.

She was flung beyond reality, as spasms of pleasure swept through her in waves, drawing him further into her, holding him fast.

Moments later, he joined her, flinging back his head, feeling his life's force spill from him into her.

They hovered there in the other-world place, the rainbow waterfall cascading over them. Then Gabe collapsed against her, spent, sated, immediately rolling onto his back and taking Sara with him. His manhood slipped free of the heated haven of her body.

Sara stayed stretched out on top of him, her head on his chest, his arms encircling her. Their breathing slowed, heartbeats quieted, but neither moved nor spoke as a magic aura surrounded them in a sensuous mist.

Finally Sara stirred but made no attempt to pull away from Gabe's arms.

"Oh, my," she said, her head still nestled on his moist chest. "That was..." Her voice trailed off.

"I don't have the words, either, Sara," he said. "It was, well, beyond description."

"Yes."

Minutes ticked away.

"Want some cold hot chocolate?" Sara said.

Gabe chuckled, causing her head to jiggle on his chest. "No, thanks. I don't plan to move an inch for at least a week. You feel like heaven right where you are, so you can't move, either."

"Oh, okay," she said, laughing softly.

Gabe began to stroke her back with one hand in a slow, steady motion that caused her to sigh with contentment.

So sleepy, she thought, stifling a yawn. She was relaxed, happy and sexually satisfied beyond her wildest imagination. She was with Gabe, and there was nowhere else she wished to be.

"Sara?"

"Mmm?"

"I know you felt very lost and confused the other night after Doc Hartman told you the truth about your father's death. But having seen you in action for the past three days as the sheriff in charge around here, it's obvious that you've gotten things squared away in your mind again."

"Gabe, I..." she started, then stopped speaking.

No, she couldn't tell him she was still in a mental quandary, confused, not knowing exactly who she was, where she was going. She didn't want to discuss all that, not now.

The lovemaking shared with Gabe had been glorious. But even more, she knew, it had been right, and she would suffer no regrets. She cared deeply for Gabriel Porter, and as long as she kept in touch with herself, made very certain she didn't step over that dangerous line and run the risks that would be unavoidable if she fell in love with him, everything would be fine.

Her relationship with Gabe was, in fact, the only section of her life that was in order and not overshadowed by the cloud of confusion.

"What I was wondering," Gabe went on, bringing her from her reverie, "is if you're back on the course you'd originally set for yourself? Added to that now, I suppose, is the decision as to whether you'll run for sheriff in the spring elections. Has all of that fallen back into place, Sara?"

He was pushing her into a corner, she thought frantically. She couldn't bare her soul to him, not again, not as she had that other night. She needed to keep her own counsel as she always had. He was waiting for an answer. She had to say *something*.

She wiggled off his body, missing him instantly, and reached for her clothes.

"Sara?"

"Yes. Yes, of course," she said, averting her eyes from his. "I have my future mapped out, remember? Etched in stone. I was momentarily thrown off kilter by what Doc Hartman told me, but that's behind me now."

"I see," Gabe said quietly, feeling a knot tighten in his gut. "Then what you're saying is that nothing has changed."

"No, Gabe," she said, slipping on her blouse, "nothing has changed."

Chapter Fourteen

The citizens of Autumn, like those of small towns across the country, turned out in mass for special events, even to the point of inventing things to celebrate. The Christmas holidays, however, were on *everyone*'s calendar, and Autumn did it up proud.

With only a few days left until the big day, the remaining hunters had headed for home. Gabe had returned to his ranch in Rio. Before leaving, he told Sara he would like to escort her to the festivities that were planned for Christmas Eve. She'd quickly agreed, finding to her amazement that she was beginning to be caught up in the buzz of holiday excitement.

On the night before Christmas, the people gathered at the town square to sing Christmas carols, each holding a lighted candle.

Jeb had been released from the hospital and received a hoot and a holler and a round of applause as he settled onto a lawn chair wrapped in a blanket. Martha stood on one side of the now-retired sheriff, and Sara and Gabe were on the other.

Gabriel Porter, Sara quickly decided, smiling inwardly, had a singing voice so terrible it could make babies cry. But, oh, it was wonderful to have him there, next to her, along with Martha and Jeb. Perfect. She was with all the people she loved, and she had a delicious, warm, fuzzy feeling inside.

All the people she *loved?* her mind echoed. Including Gabriel Porter? No! Absolutely not. She'd mentally covered that subject, had her emotions tightly under control. She was not in love, nor falling in love, with Gabe.

The songfest ended with shouts of "Merry Christmas," then to the accompaniment of squeals of excited children, a roly-poly Santa Claus lumbered across the square, a puffy pillowcase slung over one shoulder.

With a steady stream of ho-ho-ho's, Santa moved through the throng, passing out candy canes. With one last bellowing ho-ho-ho, he waved goodbye and waddled back across the square.

The crowd began to disperse with laughter and chatter ringing through the cold, clear night. Sara hugged Martha, kissed Jeb on the cheek, then Martha whisked him away.

"Hot chocolate?" Sara said, looking up at Gabe. She batted her eyelashes. "Or would you prefer cold hot chocolate?"

Gabe laughed in delight. "Lady, you're reading my mind." He slipped one arm across her shoulders. "I'll take cold hot chocolate."

"Miss Calhoun?" a voice said.

Sara turned to see Bobby and Mike Huxley standing in front of her.

"Hello," she said, smiling. "It's nice to see you both. How's your dad's leg?"

"Doc Hartman says it's mending fine," Mike said. "My dad is tired of sitting around, though." He extended a package wrapped in brown paper toward her. "Elk meat. It's not much of a thank-you for what you did for us on the Thumb, but it's good tender game."

Sara took the package. "Thank you, and please thank your folks."

"Yes, ma'am," Bobby said. "Go on, Mike, ask her."

"Ask me what?" Sara said.

"Well," Mike said, "when Sheriff Broffy was in Three C, me and Bobby went to see him. You know, to tell him we were sorry about his heart attack and all. We were talking and he said you were going to start up a Search and Rescue Back Country Unit in Autumn. Bobby and I sure would like to be a part of it."

"I see," she said.

"We discussed it with our dad, Miss Calhoun," Mike rushed on, "and he was all for it, because we're mighty grateful for what all of you did to bring us home safe. Thing is, my dad says we're kinda young for a real team. He thought..."

"Yes?" she said.

"Well, his idea was that you might consider having a junior unit, or whatever you might want to call it. You could train us, and we'd do pretend stuff, drills, whatever, until we were ready to be a part of a regular Back Country Unit. Bobby and I talked to a bunch of our friends and there's five others—one is a girl, but that's okay, I guess—that want to belong to a junior team. So, well, um, I sort of got elected as the one to ask you if you'd be willing to do it."

"My goodness," Sara said, vaguely aware that Gabe's hold on her shoulders had tightened. "This is quite a surprise."

Say no! Gabe mentally yelled. Damn it, didn't Sara see that she was overextended already? If she took on the training of a junior unit, as well as a regular one, added it to being acting sheriff, and possibly sheriff, if she decided to run for office, she wouldn't have time to breathe.

She wouldn't have time to smell the flowers.

She wouldn't have time for him.

Sara, please, say no!

"Listen," Sara said, smiling at Mike and Bobby, "give me a few days to think about this. I'll let you know right after the New Year. All right?"

"Yes, ma'am," Mike said. "We appreciate it." He jabbed his brother in the ribs with his elbow.

"Oh," Bobby said. "Yes, ma'am. Thank you, Miss Calhoun."

"Merry Christmas," Mike said. "Good night, Miss Calhoun, Mr. Porter."

"Good night," Sara and Gabe said in unison.

The boys walked away, and Sara and Gabe started toward Gabe's vehicle.

"Well, wasn't that something?" Sara said. "I'm definitely going to have to sit down and think this through. What about equipment? Insurance? What about..." She laughed. "No, I'm not dwelling on it now. We've got a date with some cold hot chocolate."

Hours later, Sara lay in bed, starring up at a ceiling she couldn't see in the darkness.

She wouldn't even bother, she decided, doing her shuffle-out-to-the-kitchen-for-warm-milk routine. Her tried-and-true remedy for not being able to sleep would be useless tonight.

She replayed in her mind once again all that had happened after she and Gabe had returned to the house.

They had made love by the tree in the rainbow waterfall of colors; exquisitely beautiful love that had left her sated and consumed with a warm glow of contentment.

But yet...

Sara shifted restlessly on the bed, frowning as she watched the movie in her mind.

There had been an energy emanating from Gabe, a nearly palpable tension. She'd asked him if something was wrong, and he'd shaken his head in the negative, producing a smile that Sara sensed was forced.

She had explained to him earlier in the week that she was taking over the duty at the sheriff's office at noon on Christmas Day to allow the other deputies to be with their families. She and Gabe could share a Christmas dinner on another day.

Gabe had seemed to understand that she had responsibilities that didn't disappear on holidays. They'd decided on him coming to Autumn Christmas morning, having a special breakfast and exchanging gifts. On her first full day off, he had said, he wanted to take her to Rio to show her his ranch.

"And meet the ever-famous Angel," she had said, laughing.

Yes, Sara mused, on the surface, if a little mouse had been watching from the corner tonight, everything would have appeared to be absolutely fine.

But there had been an undercurrent, an undefinable *something* that was causing her to register a sense of unease and keeping her from drifting off into blissful sleep.

"Sleep. Now," she ordered herself. "Santa Claus won't come if you're awake, Sara Ann Calhoun."

When she finally slept, she was once again plagued by the nightmare of being lost in the snow. Cold. So cold. And alone.

During her morning shower, Sara delivered a stern lecture to herself to forget about the gloomy thoughts regarding the previous night. For all she knew, she'd imagined that Gabe had been in a strange and unsettling mood.

It was Christmas, for heaven's sake, and glad tidings of great joy were the order of the day. She and Gabe were going to share the event and create some lovely memories.

She allowed herself to linger for a moment on the mental image of Patrick Calhoun, then smiled gently. Gabe had been right; her father would have wanted her to celebrate the holidays, to be happy and move forward with her life.

As she dried with a fluffy towel, she thought about the conversation with Mike and Bobby Huxley.

A junior Search and Rescue Unit, she mused. She'd promised them an answer to their request in a week or so. That was just dandy. She still didn't know if she wanted to establish a *regular* team, let alone take on the project the boys were eager to have.

Today, she decided, after Gabe had returned to Rio and she'd delivered gifts to Martha and Jeb, then settled in for a solitary afternoon at the sheriff's office, she'd think. Yes, she'd sort and sift, get in close touch with her inner being and determine exactly where she was headed. Good plan.

Humming "Jingle Bells," she dressed in winter-white wool slacks, a bright red sweater and brown loafers.

Glancing at her watch, she hurried to the kitchen, setting the table for breakfast with the added festive touches of red candles and green linen napkins.

When she heard the rumble of Gabe's vehicle, she went to the front door and flung it open.

"Hello," she called, smiling. "Merry Christmas."

"Merry Christmas to you, too," Gabe yelled, matching her smile.

Everything was fine, Sara thought, feeling a tingle of excitement as Gabe approached the house. They were going to have a wonderful Christmas morning together.

When Gabe entered the living room, he dropped a quick kiss on Sara's lips, then strode across the room to place a brightly wrapped gift beneath the tree. He shrugged out of his jacket, set it on a chair, then met Sara in the middle of the room.

"Now then," he said, pulling her into his arms, "let's do this Merry Christmas business properly."

"Indeed."

The kiss they shared was long, searing, igniting the embers of desire still glowing within them into leaping flames of passion. That kiss was followed by another, and yet another, each more urgent, hungry, delivering and receiving messages of burning want and need.

"Whoa," Gabe finally said, taking a ragged breath. "Halt."

"Halt?" Sara repeated, with a little puff of air.

"You have to understand, ma'am," he said, still holding her close, "that not one morsel of food has passed my lips this morning in anticipation of the scrumptious breakfast you promised would be served at this establishment."

"Ah, I see," she said, nodding. "You're in a weakened condition, starving to death, lacking the energy to jump my bones."

"Bingo," he said, chuckling. "I need food, woman."

"Yes, sir, coming right up, sir. I'll head for the kitchen, you start a fire in the hearth. Okay?"

"Got it, but cook fast."

"Oh, good grief," she said, laughing as she left the room.

Yes, she reaffirmed in her mind, everything was just fine.

The breakfast, Gabe declared over an hour later, had been even more scrumptious than promised.

Sara glowed under his praise, confessing that she'd never prepared vegetable omelets before.

Also on the menu had been crisp bacon, cinnamon rolls from Sissy's Bakery, and orange sherbet topped with fresh fruit.

"It's traditional in Autumn," she informed Gabe, "to have Sissy's cinnamon rolls on Christmas morning."

"Duly noted," Gabe said.

"More coffee?"

"No, I'm so full that I'm about to burst. I'll help you clean up the kitchen."

"Later," she said, getting to her feet. "It's time for presents."

Gabe smiled as he followed her into the living room.

Sara was so beautiful today, absolutely enchanting. Her eyes were sparkling, and there was an endearing little-girl quality to her, befitting Christmas morning.

His smile faded.

If only she would stay this open, carefree, happy and loving. But she wouldn't. He could easily picture her in his mind as she'd appear this afternoon at the sheriff's office. Her walls would be back in place, she'd be strictly business, and even the most minute section of her mind would be focused on her work.

He'd hardly slept last night, as the conversation with the Huxley boys taunted and tormented him. Somewhere in the middle of the night he realized that he was using Sara's pending decision regarding a junior Search and Rescue Unit as an emotional measuring stick.

If Sara took on that project, in addition to everything else she was doing, he would be defeated. He would have failed in his attempt to teach her the importance of stopping to smell the flowers. And he would have to face the cold realization that there was simply no room in Sara's life for him.

She would be stating loud and clear by her actions that she refused to run the risks involved in loving, falling in love, being in love.

He would have lost Sara to her own fears before they'd even had a chance to discover what they might have had together in the future.

"Gabe?"

"What? Oh, I'm sorry, I was woolgathering." He sat down on the sofa.

Sara handed him a festively wrapped gift, then sat down next to him. They exchanged smiles, then Gabe began to tear away the paper.

"Hey now," he said as the gift was revealed. "This is sensational, Sara."

"I hope you like it."

She had given him a man's jewelry box that had been intricately carved by hand on the sides, depicting geese in flight. The wood was a rich, warm brown and satin smooth to the touch. The inside of the box was lined with navy blue velvet.

Gabe balanced the box in one hand, slid the other to the nape of her neck and kissed her deeply.

"Thank you," he said. "It's a great present. I'll cherish it, Sara, I truly will." He glanced over at the tree. "Want me to bring you your gift?"

"I'll get it," she said, jumping to her feet and laughing. "Are you impressed with my mature behavior? I adore presents." She hurried to the tree and returned to sit next to him with the gift on her lap.

A wave of trepidation swept through Gabe, and he frowned.

Had he made a mistake when he'd chosen this gift for Sara? he wondered. Well, it was too late now. What was done, was done.

Sara removed the outer wrapping to discover a lidded box beneath. She lifted off the cover, put it to one side, then slowly, carefully, brushed back the tissue beneath.

"Oh," she whispered, instant tears misting her eyes.

It was a doll. It was a beautiful baby doll, with curly yellow hair and a gorgeous lavender organdy dress. A tiny cluster of silk, lily of the valley flowers was attached to the center of the satin ribbon encircling the waistline.

With trembling hands, Sara gently, very gently, lifted the doll from the box and watched her eyes open to reveal sapphire blue ones.

But Sara knew they would be blue, because this was...

"Rosalie," she said. "Oh, Gabe, it's Rosalie."

She turned to look at him, tears glistening in her eyes. "Thank you. I really don't know what to say to make you understand how much this means to me. Thank you so very, very much."

"I *do* understand," he said, smiling. "And you're very welcome."

And at that moment, Gabriel Porter knew that he was deeply in love with Sara Ann Calhoun.

Chapter Fifteen

Gabe blinked as the full impact of what he'd just acknowledged as truth hit him with as much force as a powerful blow to the solar plexus.

He was in love with Sara.

To his own dismay, he realized that he didn't know if he should whoop with glee or sink his head into his hands in despair.

But as he watched Sara wrap her arms around Rosalie and hug the baby doll, tears still shining in Sara's eyes, Gabriel Porter was filled with the greatest joy he had ever known.

"Sara..."

She put the doll carefully in the box, then turned to look at Gabe.

"Sensitivity," she said, managing a small smile. "That's what you have, Gabe. The beautiful quality, the gift of sensitivity. I witnessed it when you interacted with Mavis Huxley, and when, well, it's always there. I felt so foolish that day on Thinker's Thumb when I told you about Rosalie, but now here she is, so special, so lovely, and mine. Thank you."

Gabe started to reply, then realized that an achy sensation had gripped his throat, making it impossible to speak. As he struggled to gain control of his raging emotions, he nodded and caressed Sara's cheek with his thumb.

"Merry Christmas, Sara Ann," he finally managed to say, his voice husky.

"Merry Christmas, Gabriel," she whispered.

Their eyes met, and time seemed to stop.

He had a major battle on his hands, Gabe knew, to break down Sara's walls for all time. She cared for him, he was positive of that. She might even be in love with him, but he'd bet his last dime that she would refuse to admit that, even to herself.

Patience, Porter. That's what it was going to take to win the love of Sara. Yes, patience, the sensitivity she'd spoken of, and proof that if she would run the risk of loving him, she wouldn't end up with a broken heart. She wouldn't be alone and lonely.

Lord, he wanted to tell her how he felt, shout it from the rooftops.

Patience, Porter.

Sara was like a skittish fawn, ready to dash away and seek the safety behind her walls at the slightest hint of what she might consider danger. His declaration of love at this point would cause her to bolt for cover.

Somehow, he had to make her see that what they could have together would be glorious. He had to guide her, gently, from her path that focused on nothing but her career, on work, work, work.

Oh, yes, he was facing a battle, but he would be victorious. He just had to be.

"Well," Sara said, tearing her gaze from Gabe's, "the morning is flying by. I want to deliver my gifts to Martha and Jeb before I report in to the office. Would you like to visit them with me?"

Gabe nodded. "Yes, I have presents for them, too."

"Let's go in separate vehicles, then I can drive directly to the office from the Broffys'." She set the box holding the baby doll on the coffee table. "I need to change into my uniform." She got to her feet.

"Sara, wait," Gabe said. He stood as she turned to face him. "One more thing."

"Yes?"

Without speaking further, he drew her close and kissed her deeply. When he finally released her, Sara hoped her trembling legs would carry her down the hall so she could change her clothes.

In her bedroom, she sank onto the edge of the bed and placed one hand on her racing heart.

Gabriel Porter, her mind hummed. He constantly added to her inner turmoil and confusion. She was a mental mess, a total wreck.

She shook her head in self-disgust, then stood and began to remove her clothing.

Rosalie. She didn't care if it was ridiculous for a twenty-five-year-old woman to be moved to tears over receiving a baby doll for Christmas. She was thrilled with her gift. So be it.

What was unsettling was the rush of emotions still assaulting her because it had been Gabe who had given her the doll. Gabe, who had not just listened that day in the tent on Thinker's Thumb, but had *heard* her lifelong yearning for a pretty doll. Gabe, who had touched a place deep within her heart.

And she was terrified.

When she was dressed in her uniform, Sara took a steadying breath, squared her shoulders, lifted her chin and left the bedroom.

"All set?" she said breezily as she reentered the living room.

"I unplugged the tree lights," Gabe said. "We didn't clean up the kitchen, Sara."

"No matter. I'll do it when I get home tonight. I don't want to be late reporting in to relieve Dale."

"No, of course not," he said quietly. "Duty calls."

Sara looked at him questioningly for a moment, then spun around.

"I'll get my jacket," she said, "then we're off to play Santa Claus at Martha and Jeb's."

"Right," he said, reaching for his jacket.

Patience, Porter, he told himself. Patience.

Jeb was in a chipper mood, and to Sara's amazement and delight had the brochures for the cruise he and Martha would take spread out on the coffee table.

After greetings of Merry Christmas accompanied by hugs, Jeb proceeded to inform Sara and Gabe of the exact route of the ship, which ports they would stop at along the way and the list of on-board activities available. Martha Broffy simply smiled, albeit a tad smugly.

The four exchanged gifts, and the appropriate oohs and aahs and thank-yous were expressed. Martha passed out crystal cups filled with homemade eggnog.

"So, Sara Ann," Jeb said, "are you going to run for sheriff in the spring?"

Gabe tensed, his eyes riveted on Sara.

"Spring is a long way off, Jeb," she said. "Martha, this eggnog is delicious as always."

"Did the Huxley boys track you down?" Jeb asked. "They're all charged up about joining your Search and Rescue Back Country Unit."

"Yes, they spoke to me. Hux suggested I start a junior unit for the younger group. They could work their way up to a regular team."

Jeb nodded. "Interesting idea. What did you tell them?"

"That I'd give them an answer right after the New Year rolls in."

"Mercy, Sara Ann," Martha said, "if you take on all of that you'll have to make an appointment with yourself to have time to sneeze."

"That's a fact," Jeb said.

"Amen," Gabe muttered.

"It took a heart attack to make me see the light, Sara Ann," Jeb said. He swept one hand above the cruise brochures. "There's more to life than working." He smiled over at Martha. "A lot more."

Martha matched his smile. "You're a randy old coot, Jeb Broffy."

"You bet I am, Martha Broffy," he said, chuckling, "and I love you, darlin'."

"Hush with you now," Martha said, blushing prettily. She looked at Gabe. "So, Gabriel, how was your Christmas tree crop? Did you sell all that you cut?"

Sara listened absently as Gabe reported on the tree sales and began to explain how he'd reached the point of having a generous number ready to cut each year, with varying sizes coming up behind for the future. When he went on to how many acres of land he allowed to rest for a predetermined length of time, she tuned out what he was saying.

Martha and Jeb were so deeply in love, Sara mused. She'd accepted that fact as a given all of her life, never really dwelling on it. They had always been Martha and Jeb, together, as they should be.

But she was viewing the Broffys today with fresh eyes, as though seeing them for the first time. Through many, many years they'd stood by each other, always there, in good times and bad.

They had just weathered the scare of Jeb's heart attack, and were preparing with enthusiasm for the next phase of their lives.

Jeb Broffy had been a hardworking and dedicated sheriff of Autumn and Canyon County for over three decades. But he had not, Sara now realized, ever lost track of his personal priorities, of the important role Martha played in his life. With no embarrassment, dear sweet Jeb had looked at his beloved wife and said "I love you, darlin'."

Jeb and Martha Broffy had run the risk of loving, falling in love, being in love with each other. They'd found a balance between work and play, career and home, and made it all work. What they had together was beautiful.

Sara shifted her gaze to Gabe, hearing Jeb ask him a question about one of Gabe's horses, then savoring the deep rumble of Gabe's voice as he replied.

Do you know the difference between being alone and being lonely?

Gabe's words echoed in Sara's mind once again, but this time she allowed them to stay front row center instead of pushing them angrily away.

She stared at Gabe, looked at Martha and Jeb again, then back to Gabe.

Gabe had been trying over and over to tell her what Martha and Jeb had discovered many years ago; there had to be time to stop and smell the flowers. There had to be a healthy balance. There had to be room for more than just work, or a person would run the risk of alone becoming lonely.

But, oh, dear, loving was a tremendous risk, too!

"Sara," Gabe said, "are you keeping track of what time it is?"

"What?" she said, jerking in her chair. "Oh, I'm sorry, I was hypnotized by the flames of the fire in the hearth." She looked at her watch, then got to her feet. "Goodness, I've got to get to the office."

In a flurry of putting on jackets, giving hugs goodbye, and more wishes of Merry Christmas, Sara and Gabe left the Broffys' house.

Outside, Gabe kissed Sara deeply, told her he'd call her that night, and they drove away in separate vehicles.

It was a weary Sara Ann Calhoun who sat curled up in her father's chair that night in the glow of the Christmas tree lights. She was wearing her comfortable old velour robe and black-and-white polka dot socks, and a fire crackled in the hearth.

The telephone had not rung once at the sheriff's office during the seemingly endless afternoon. Yet, when Randy had shown up to relieve her, she had been exhausted.

Heavy thinking, she mused, sipping a mug of hot chocolate, wore out more than a person's brain. She was physically tired, too, as though she'd spent the time tromping up and down Thinker's Thumb.

But the tedious hours had been worth the effort. She was far from having all the answers to her multitude of questions, but a few of the long list of issues to address were beginning to seem less ominous. There was a tiny speck of light at the end of the dark tunnel of confusion. It wasn't great, but it was certainly better than nothing.

She glanced at the telephone, recalling the earlier conversation with Gabe, a lovely, soft smile forming on her lips.

She would be off duty the day after tomorrow, she'd informed Gabe, and plans were made for him to pick her up for a day at his ranch.

"Yes, ma'am," he had said, "it's time you came to Heaven's Gate."

Sara drained the mug, then set it on the small table next to Patrick's chair.

Heaven's Gate, she mentally repeated. That was the name of Gabe's ranch. It was also his Search and Rescue team's code for "All is well, the mission has been accomplished."

Heaven's Gate. She yearned to be able to get her life in order, know exactly who she was, what she wanted, where she was going. She wanted, oh, how she needed, to be able to look at her reflection in the mirror and be able to say with conviction, "Sara Ann Calhoun, you, yourself, the woman, are at Heaven's Gate."

She would accomplish that goal.

"I just have to, Rosalie," she whispered to the baby doll, which lay in the box beneath the Christmas tree. "Somehow."

The morning of the scheduled trip to Rio dawned clear and very cold. Dressed in jeans, a powder blue cable-knit sweater, and fleece-lined indoor-outdoor calf-high boots, Sara listened to a weather report on the radio while she ate breakfast.

A storm-watch was in effect for Yavapai, Copper and Canyon Counties until further notice, the announcer said. A storm front was approaching, which promised several inches of snow accompanied by high winds. Due to unstable conditions, it was too early in the day to determine exactly what direction the blizzard would take. The listeners were urged to stay tuned to that station for more information as it became available.

Sara got to her feet and went to the kitchen window, gazing up at the blue sky.

Well, she decided, she'd informed the deputy on duty at the office where she could be reached, Gabe would be keeping track of the weather because of his role as a Search and Rescue team leader, and that was that. There was certainly no point in canceling her plans over what might, or might not, happen regarding the weather later in the day.

When Gabe arrived to pick her up, Sara was so incredibly glad to see him it was impossible to hide her smile, or quell the desire that swirled within her as she returned his kiss of greeting in total abandon.

There was a current of sensuality, of passion, awareness, want and need, that literally crackled through the air.

The drive to Rio was delightful. They talked, laughed and argued loudly over the merits of a bestselling novel they'd both read.

The lack of traffic and the snow-free roads made it possible for them to reach Rio in just under thirty minutes, and to arrive at Gabe's ranch ten minutes later.

Sara's eyes were sparkling as Gabe turned onto a gravel driveway that led to a house in the distance. Beyond the house was a red barn, and half a dozen smaller buildings. Several horses grazed in corrals surrounded by pristine white fences.

Gabe was acutely aware of the fact that he was suddenly extremely tense. His hold on the steering wheel had tightened, and he slid frequent glances at Sara, trying to gauge her reactions as they came closer and closer to the house.

He felt like a teenager on his first date, he silently fumed, trying to impress the pretty cheerleader. But, damn it, he was in love with this woman sitting next to him. She was seeing for the first time what he hoped would be her future home, the place where she would stay by his side as his wife.

Oh, Lord, he wanted to tell her how he felt, what his hopes and dreams for the tomorrows were, how he eagerly anticipated the day when their children's laughter would ring through the air.

Not yet, Porter, he told himself. He mustn't say anything yet. Remember... *patience*.

"Sara," he said quietly, "welcome to Heaven's Gate."

The house was a single-story ranch-style, typical of the West, and was constructed of red brick. It had three bedrooms, a large living room, a sunny kitchen with dining space set into a bay window area, and a small room off the living room that Gabe referred to as his den.

The furniture was mismatched, massive and looked deliciously comfortable. The earth tones gave the house a warm, cozy atmosphere, and Sara was enchanted.

"Oh, Gabe," she said after the conducted tour, "it's wonderful. This house—no, this *home*—suits you perfectly. I can definitely understand why you're content here."

But would *she* be content here? his mind yelled.

"I'm glad you like it," he said, smiling.

She swept her gaze over the living room again. "Oh, I do, I truly do. That fireplace is gorgeous." She paused. "Where's Angel?"

Gabe chuckled. "There's a new litter of kittens in the barn and, well, you see, Sara, Angel has a bit of an identity crisis. Every time there are new kittens, Angel appoints herself the official nanny or something. She stays close, helps give the bunch baths, the whole nine yards. Even *I* can't compete with newborn kittens."

"How marvelous," Sara said, laughing in delight. "May we go to the barn, see the kittens, and Mother Angel?" She grasped one of Gabe's hands and tugged. "Come on, Gabe. Please?"

He would follow her to the end of the earth, he thought, if it meant he could win her love.

"Sure," he said, matching her smile, "we're off to the barn."

She was at Gabe's Heaven's Gate, Sara thought, as they went out the kitchen door, but for a few stolen hours she was going to pretend that it was *her* Heaven's Gate, too. She was going to pretend that her mission was accomplished and all was well.

Chapter Sixteen

Gabe's spirits soared higher with each step he and Sara took toward the barn. As she swept her gaze over the view, she began to bombard him with questions regarding the ranch.

What is that building? And that one over there? Where are the cattle? Are the Christmas trees beyond that hill? The horses are gorgeous. Do you like to ride? How many men work for you? Do they live in the bunkhouse? Your home is immaculate. Do you have a housekeeper? How many kittens are there in the barn?

"Whoa," Gabe finally said, laughing and raising both hands as he quit walking. "Your questions are getting ahead of my answers."

Sara stopped and smiled up at him. "Sorry. It's just so fascinating, all of it. This certainly is a different way of life from being a fast-lane lawyer."

"There's no comparison, Sara," he said, his smile fading. "My priorities are entirely different now. I've learned to—"

"Yes, I know," she interrupted, a slight edge to her voice. "You've learned to stop and smell the flowers. You're beginning to sound like a broken record on that subject, Gabe."

He gripped her shoulders and looked directly into her eyes. "Yes, I suppose I am, but that's because I feel so strongly about it. I don't want you to pay the price that I did for having tunnel vision about my career. I want..." Damn it, he wanted to marry her, spend the rest of his life with her, because he loved her. Patience, patience, patience, Porter. "Look, let's back up here a bit, shall we?"

"To where?" she said, frowning.

"Well, let's see, where were we? Oh, yes. I have a housekeeper who comes in twice a week. She lives in Rio, and will be showing up in time to fix us lunch later. Some of the men live here, but most are out of Rio. That second bunkhouse is empty. And there are four newborn kittens in the barn." He dropped a quick kiss on her lips. "Okay?"

Sara looked at him for a long moment, then nodded and smiled. "Okay."

They started off again, and Gabe slid one arm across her shoulders.

"One bunkhouse is empty," Sara repeated thoughtfully. "Gabe, an idea just flashed into my mind. A camp. What if I held training sessions for a junior Search and Rescue team in a camp environment? It could be done on selected weekends during the school year, and maybe two or three weeks at a stretch in the summer." She paused. "Hey, listen to me. I'm taking over your ranch, just filled up your empty bunkhouse with a teenage would-be Search and Rescue team. You're a pushy person, Sara Calhoun." She laughed and shook her head.

The knot that had tightened in Gabe's stomach as Sara had chattered on was so painful he grimaced.

"You're..." he started, then cleared his throat. "You're definitely going to form a junior unit?"

Sara nodded. "I admittedly don't have *all* my plans for the future mapped out, but that one, I now realize, is a given. It's an exciting project. There are a zillion details to work out, but I'll take them one at a time and find solutions to the problems that a junior team would produce."

They had reached the barn, and Gabe absently introduced Sara to two men who were coming out as he and Sara stepped inside. In the barn, he pointed to a stall strewn with hay, where a tan-and-black German shepherd lay next to a black-and-white cat. Four little bundles of fur were busily having brunch.

Sara hurried forward and dropped to her knees at the edge of the stall, slowly extending one hand toward the dog, who sniffed it, then gave it a sloppy lick.

"Hello, Angel," Sara said. "What a lovely family you have." Angel's tail thumped on the hay. "Hello, Mama Cat. What's her name, Gabe?"

"What? Oh, the cat? Her name is Dog. She's as mixed up about her identity as Angel is. Whenever she has a litter of kittens, she *expects* Angel to help out."

Sara laughed in delight, then gently drew one fingertip along the soft body of one of the kittens.

"Hurry and eat, babies," she said, "so I can have a better look at you."

Gabe stood behind Sara and dragged both hands down his face.

Dear Lord, his mind thundered, he'd lost. There was nowhere to go, nowhere to hide, from the truth, the realization that he'd lost the battle to win Sara's heart. He'd lost her to herself, to her ambition, her career tunnel vision.

He'd needed *something* to gauge his progress in his quest, and his emotional measuring stick was Sara's decision regarding the junior Search and Rescue team. On top of everything else she was involved in, she was actually going to take on more.

The bottom had just fallen out of his world.

His size, strength, intelligence meant nothing.

He'd fought a tough battle, and he'd lost.

And it hurt like hell.

He stared down at Sara where she knelt in front of him.

She was there, so close, he mused dismally, yet she was beyond his reach. He loved her so damn much, but all his hopes, dreams, fantasies, had just been smashed to smithereens.

Sara picked up one of the kittens in both hands and lifted it to eye level. The baby stuck all four paws straight out, and a tip of a tiny pink tongue poked from its mouth. The kitten was all white except for one black ear.

"You are an adorable little girl," Sara said to the kitten. "Your ever-so-fashionable choice of a hat for your ear is very snazzy. That's what I would call you if you were mine. Snazzy."

"You can have her," Gabe said, attempting to force some animation into his voice. "She'll be ready to leave Dog and Angel in about five or six weeks."

"Oh, don't tempt me," she said, putting the kitten back in the hay. Angel began to give it a bath. "I'm not sure it would be fair of me to take her, because she'd be alone so much. I don't spend all that much time at home."

No joke, Gabe fumed, knowing there was a bitter edge to his thoughts. And once she took on the junior unit, she'd probably have to carry a map so she'd remember how to get to her house.

"But she's so-o-o sweet," Sara went on. "Well, I have time to think about it."

But *he'd* run out of time, Gabe thought. Sara Ann Calhoun was not going to be his. Damn it to hell, he'd lost!

A man came running into the barn, and Gabe turned as he heard the rushing footsteps.

"Gabe," the man said, "a call just came in for you. I took it in the tack room. That storm that was due, hit right on the border of Yavapai and Copper Counties. It's big, gone to whiteout already. There's a troop leader with four Boy Scouts somewhere up in the Juniper Mountains. They want your Back Country Unit to team up with the one from Yavapai County."

"Thanks, Reggie," Gabe said, then took off running toward the barn door.

"Wait a minute," Sara yelled, attempting to scramble to her feet. She slipped on the loose hay and landed with a thud on her bottom. "Blast." She tried again, succeeded, then ran after Gabe. "Damn you, Gabriel Porter, wait for me."

When Sara literally flew through the kitchen door of the house, Gabe was nowhere in sight. She hurried into the living room, then stopped. When she heard the low rumble of Gabe's voice, she crossed the room and entered his den.

Gabe sat with his back to her in front of a sending-and-receiving radio assembled on a table on the far wall. He had a pair of earphones in place, and was holding a microphone in one hand.

Sara marched across the room to stand directly behind him.

"That's a roger," Gabe said into the microphone. "See you guys in about fifteen minutes. Over and out." He flicked several switches on the radio, then removed the earphones.

Sara cleared her throat.

Gabe snapped his head around at the unexpected noise, then got to his feet to face her.

"I lucked out," he said. "All of my team members were within earshot of their radios. I covered it in one call. They'll come here, load their gear into my vehicle, and we'll be on our way. I'll have one of my hands drive you back to Autumn."

Sara planted her fists on her hips and narrowed her eyes.

"You certainly will not. This is me, Sara, remember? I'm trained and certified in Search and Rescue. I'm going with you."

"No," he said, moving around her and starting toward the door, "you're not."

"Hold it right there, mister."

Gabe stopped, turned and folded his arms tightly over his chest. Sara crossed the room to stand in front of him.

"You're out of your mind, Gabriel," she said, frowning up at him. "From what Reggie said in the barn, it's obvious that you need all the manpower you can get. *I...am...going...with...you.*"

Gabe shook his head. "Forget it, Sara Ann. I'm Incident Commander. Whenever we work with the Yavapai County Back Country Unit, that's my role. So, as the one in charge, I'm telling you that you're not going on this search."

"Why not?"

"Because, ma'am," he said, matching her frown, "you don't have the proper equipment with you. Your boots are pretty, but they're not worth squat when it comes to climbing, or trekking through heavy, wet snow. Your jacket is adequate for an outing to visit my ranch, but it won't keep you warm enough for long enough in the Juniper Mountains."

"Oh."

"Yeah... oh. End of story."

"No, it's not. Listen to me. So, all right, I won't be able to stay out as long as the rest of the team. I concede that."

"How magnanimous of you," he said, rolling his eyes heavenward.

"Would you quit being such a pain in the butt and listen to me?" she said, none too quietly.

"There's nothing you can say that will—"

"Shut up, Porter. I can read sign as good, if not better, than anyone on your team. I'll know how to proceed with whatever method of search you choose to use. For as long as I'm able to stay out there, I'll be an asset to your unit, and you know it."

"You're forgetting one very important fact."

"Which is?"

"Without the proper equipment, you'll have to head back to base camp long before the rest of us. Alone, Sara. You'll have to return from wherever we are *alone*."

"I'm aware of that."

"Oh, really? Don't you think that's rather *risky?*" he said, a biting edge to his voice.

"Yes, I suppose it is risky, but taking certain risks goes along with being a part of a Search and Rescue Unit. That's no news flash. What is your problem, Gabe? You've got a chip on your shoulder from here to Toledo. What are you so angry about?"

Emotions were churning within Gabe like a boiling caldron of frustration, pain, disappointment and more, erupting before he could even attempt to keep them under his control.

His hands shot out to grip Sara's shoulders, and a pulse beat wildly in his temple. Sara stared up at him with wide eyes.

"What is my problem?" he said. "I'll tell you exactly what my problem is, lady, so listen up. My problem is you, Miss Sara Ann Calhoun."

"Me?" she shot back. "What in the hell did *I* do?"

"You came into my life, and knocked me over, turned me inside out. At first, I saw you as a mirror image of myself when I lived and worked in Los Angeles. I decided to save you from yourself, noble bastard that I am, and teach you the importance of stopping to smell the flowers.

"But then, Sara? Little by little, you staked your claim on me. You'd come out from behind those damnable walls of yours long enough to weave more of your spell, then dash for cover again."

"I—"

"No, Sara. I waited, watched, hoped...hell, *I prayed*, that you would see the light, realize that your tunnel vision regarding your career was wrong, so damn wrong. I wanted, needed, you to recognize that fact not only for yourself, but for me, too. Why?"

He drew a ragged breath, and his voice was raspy when he spoke again.

"Because, Sara Ann, I fell in love with you."

"What?" she whispered.

"Oh, you heard right. I love you, Sara. Lord, I had such dreams for our future together. I wanted you to become my wife, my other half, the mother of my children. I wanted you to live here with me, at *our* Heaven's Gate, for the rest of our lives.

"But you had so much on your agenda, and today when you said you were going ahead with starting a junior Search and Rescue team, I knew I'd lost my battle. That's what it was, Sara, a fight to win your love over the lure of your career. I lost."

"Gabe..."

"Why am I angry on top of all the other emotions that are tearing me apart?" he went on. "Risks. It's the risks, Sara, the ones you're willing to take. I have to respect that you're ready to go on this search, to give your expertise for as long as you're able, then run the risk of going back to base camp alone. I'd do the same thing myself, under the circumstances.

"But what I'm mad as hell about is that you're not willing to run any risks on a personal plane. You're so damn afraid of being hurt by loving someone, by loving *me*, that you scramble behind your walls the moment I get too close. You're not just hiding from me, Sara, you're hiding from yourself, too.

"I love you, Sara Ann, but as of right now, I'm done, finished, I quit. I know when I'm beat. You're not going on this search even for a shorter time than the rest of us, because I need to have my total concentration centered on the mission. I can't do that if you're there. Not today. Go home, Sara."

He dropped his hands from her shoulders, then turned and started toward the door. In the doorway, he stopped and looked at her again over one shoulder.

"I can't help wondering, though," he said, his voice gritty with emotion, "if you ever discovered the difference between being alone and being lonely." He paused. "Goodbye, Sara Ann."

And then he was gone.

A shiver coursed through Sara as she stared at the empty doorway, and she wrapped her hands around her elbows.

"Gabe?" she said, an echo of threatening tears in her voice.

On trembling legs, she moved to the closest chair and sank onto it, keeping her arms encircling her protectively.

Gabe's passionately spoken words tumbled through her mind like a wild river out of control, slamming one into the next to create a cacophony of unbearable volume.

She pressed shaking fingertips to her temples and closed her eyes, willing herself not to cry.

Gabriel Porter was in love with her, her mind hammered unmercifully. Gabe loved her, but before she could even fully comprehend what that meant to her, he had walked out of her life, pain radiating from the depths of his dark eyes. Pain that *she* had caused him.

"Oh, Gabe," she whispered.

Such harsh accusations he'd hurled at her. She wasn't just hiding from him behind her walls, she was hiding from herself, as well? She was willing to take risks in the arena of Search and Rescue, but was too cowardly to run risks as a woman? Did she yet know the difference between being alone and being lonely?

Gabriel Porter was in love with her.

He had, she knew, touched her heart in a way no other man ever had. But each time she had crept closer to tentatively consider examining the new and unsettling emotions he evoked within her, she'd been too frightened to go further, to seek the answers to her multitude of questions.

Dear God, had all of Gabe's accusations been true?

Just under an hour later, Sara entered her house, having been driven to Autumn by Reggie, who had given up attempting to make small talk with Sara ten minutes after leaving Rio.

Sara walked slowly forward, feeling so drained, so totally exhausted, it was difficult to put one foot in front of the other. She stopped at the Christmas tree, her gaze falling on the baby doll in the box beneath.

Picking up Rosalie, Sara hugged her close, buried her face in the doll's silky curls and wept.

Chapter Seventeen

Hours later, Sara rotated her neck back and forth, making certain she didn't disturb the position of the earphones she wore.

After a loud, long cry that had accomplished nothing more than giving her a roaring headache, red nose and puffy eyes, she'd driven to Martha and Jeb's.

Without giving them an explanation for her appearance and gratefully knowing they wouldn't press for details, Sara asked Jeb if he knew the radio frequency for the Yavapai and Copper County Search and Rescue Back Country Units when on a combined-team mission. Jeb answered in the affirmative.

May she please, Sara had gone on, close herself up in their den where she wouldn't disturb them, and listen to the transmissions between the search team and the base camp?

"Yep," Jeb had said.

Settling onto the chair in front of the radio, Sara had begun her vigil.

Communication between the searchers and their base camp was infrequent, and she hung on every word, able to trace their progress in the Juniper Mountains on the map on the wall above the radio.

As the Incident Commander, it was Gabe's voice she heard reporting into the base camp. Gabe's deep, rich, masculine voice.

Gabriel Porter—the man who loved her.

Gabriel Porter, who had caused her to weep yet find no answers to the ever-growing list of questions tormenting her, allowing confusion to reign supreme in her befuddled mind.

Gabriel Porter, who had walked in, now out, of her life, having irrevocably changed it for all time.

There was a sharp knock at the closed door of the room, bringing Sara from her troubled thoughts.

"Yes, come in," she said.

Martha entered carrying a tray, pushing the door closed behind her. Sara slid one of the earpieces up so she would be able to hear Martha, but left the other in place.

"I brought you some hot stew and fresh bread," Martha said, putting the tray next to the radio. "Do you know how many hours you've been in here, Sara Ann? It's nearly five o'clock."

"I know," Sara said. "They're running out of daylight on the search, and they haven't found the Scouts. At least the snow didn't start up again after that initial storm this morning."

"Eat," Martha said, pointing to the tray.

Sara moved her chair over a bit to enable her to reach the food, while still holding the one earphone in place. Martha pulled up another chair and sat down.

"Would you like to talk about it now, Sara Ann?" Martha said gently. "You'd obviously had a good cry before you came over here, which we women are wise enough to do when the need arises."

"My crying jag didn't help a bit," Sara said. She took a spoonful of stew, only then realizing how hungry she was. "Thank you for the supper, Martha. It's delicious."

"You're welcome. What's troubling you, dear?"

Sara sighed. "Gabe."

"Really? Well, my stars, that doesn't make much sense. Having seen the two of you together, it's as clear as a pig in a poke that he's in love with you, and you're in love with him. That doesn't sound like trouble to me."

Sara nearly choked on the second spoonful of stew. Martha reached over and gave her a solid whack on the back.

"Thanks, I think," Sara muttered.

"So? Go on with your story."

"*You're* telling it, not me. I never said I was in love with Gabe."

"My dear child, I have two perfectly good eyes. Well, they're perfectly good if I wear my bifocals. I know love when I see it, for mercy's sake." Martha paused and tapped one fingertip against her chin. "Perhaps the person you didn't tell about your love for Gabriel was Miss Sara Ann Calhoun, herself. Yes, that has possibilities. I can clearly imagine how the idea of having fallen in love with Gabe could scare the britches off you. Oh, that sounded rather naughty. Anyway, you get my point."

"Don't be silly. Why would loving Gabe frighten me?" Sara said, attempting to sound nonchalant and failing miserably.

"Because love hasn't been kindly to you, Sara Ann. Your mama, Patrick...then old Jeb up and has a heart attack. To add to the jumble, love between a man and woman is very different than the love you have for parents and dear friends. It's more intense, comes from a secret place in your heart and soul. The joy is richer, but the hurt, if it happens, is so very painful. Darling, are you in love with Gabriel?"

Quick tears filled Sara's eyes. "I don't know, Martha. I just don't know. I'm so confused. Gabe said that he loves me, but he's staying away from me, keeping out of my life from now on because he lost me to my career and...and to my own fears."

"Is he right?"

"No. Yes." Sara threw up her hands. *"I don't know."*

"Sara Ann, why have you sat in that hard-backed chair for the major portion of this day with no signs showing that you're leaving?"

"Martha, for Pete's sake, Gabe is out there," she said, waving a finger at the map on the wall. "It could snow again at any moment, it's rough terrain, they must all be exhausted by now, and... How can you ask such a question? I'm not budging from this crummy chair until I know that Gabe is safely back at the base camp."

"Oh, I see," Martha said, getting to her feet. "That doesn't make much sense to me, either."

"Why not? Didn't you wait up for Jeb whenever he went out on a late call during all those years he was sheriff?"

"Yes, of course I did, but I'm in love with Jeb Broffy."

"And I'm in love with Gabriel Porter," Sara yelled.

"Hell's fire, Sara Ann," Jeb hollered, through the wall, "that's not a news bulletin. Any fool looking at you knows that."

"Having a heart attack didn't harm the man's hearing, or his lungs," Martha said thoughtfully, staring at the wall.

"Cut," Sara said, slicing one hand through the air. "Stop. Halt." She placed one hand on her heart, took a deep breath, then let it out slowly. "There. I'm calm. I'm fine."

"You're in love," Martha said, beaming.

"I'm having a nervous breakdown!"

"Love feels like that at times," Martha said, nodding.

"Martha?" Sara said, her voice unsteady. "I don't know if I *want* to be in love, but the thought of never seeing Gabe again, of never... Oh, Lord, I'm still so confused."

"Give it some time, sweet girl. This is all brand new to you."

"I do love him, Martha," Sara said softly. "I can't hide from that fact any longer."

"I know, dear, I know."

Suddenly Sara grabbed the other earpiece and set it firmly in place, holding the headset on her ears with both hands.

"Another storm is sweeping into that area, and it's snowing heavily," she said. "Wait... there's static on the line but... it's going to whiteout nearly as fast as it's falling."

"Mercy's sake," Martha said, folding her hands beneath her chin.

A few minutes later, Martha went to get Jeb, and the pair stood side by side, watching Sara intently. Twenty long, silent minutes passed with no transmission coming over the radio, Sara straining her ears for the slightest sound.

Sara stiffened. "There's a crackling noise like someone is trying to transmit." She paused, then whispered, "Come on, Gabe, let me hear your beautiful voice. Speak to me, Gabriel."

Martha reached for Jeb's hand.

"Oh, God," Sara said, the color draining from her face.

"Sara Ann?" Jeb said. "What is it, girl? What's going on out there?"

She looked at Martha and Jeb, a stricken expression on her face.

"They've found the Scouts and their leader," Sara said, her voice trembling, "and they're heading back to base camp because it's getting very dark. But..." Tears filled her eyes. "But Moses is reporting in. It's Moses, not Gabe. They lost contact with Gabe. They don't know where he is, and they're coming in because it's too dark to look further. They're coming in without Gabe." Two tears slid down her cheeks as she removed the earphones and turned off the radio.

"Easy does it now," Jeb said quietly. "You know the basic rules of Search and Rescue. A search team should not put their own lives in jeopardy unless a child is lost. To hike the Junipers in a snowstorm at night would be mighty foolish. Gabe is not a child. What's more, he's a trained Search and Rescue man. He knows how to take care of himself out there."

Sara got to her feet. "He can't take care of himself if he's injured, hurt in some way that makes it impossible for him to do what's necessary to be able to survive the night in those mountains."

"You don't know that he's hurt, Sara Ann," Jeb said.

"I don't know that he isn't, either!"

"That's true," Jeb said, nodding. "Being injured is a risk every member of a Search and Rescue team takes whenever they go out on a mission."

"I'm very aware of that," Sara said, beginning to pace back and forth across the small room. "Those risks are very clear to me. I understand them, I'm comfortable with them. You climb a mountain, you might fall off. It's very simple."

Martha and Jeb exchanged a concerned look as they heard the bitter-sounding edge to Sara's voice.

"Big, brave Sara Ann," she went on, with a snort of self-disgust. "I came back to Autumn to right the wrong. Search and rescue? Hey, I'm a pro, academy certified, I'll have you know. Take on the risks involved in being in charge of a Search and Rescue Unit? You bet. No problem. I'm not afraid of anything that's out there."

"Sara Ann, don't," Martha said.

Sara spun around to face them, tears tracking her pale cheeks. "Except life. I'm scared to death of life, living it to the fullest by running the risk of loving and being loved in return." A sob caught in her throat. "I lost the love of Gabriel Porter because of my fears. I hurt him so badly, and he's out of my reach now."

"Honey..." Martha said.

"It's my own fault," Sara said. "I have no one to blame but myself. I can't have Gabe in my future because I'm too late coming to grips with my past, just too late. But, by damn, there's one last thing I can do before I start facing all the tomorrows without him."

"What?" Jeb said. "What are you planning to do?"

"I'm going to find him, Jeb. I'll cover every inch of the Junipers if I have to, but I'm going to find Gabriel Porter."

Chapter Eighteen

Two hours later, Sara parked next to the last vehicle in the row in front of Gabe's house and turned off the ignition.

The house was ablaze with light, and she whispered the fervent hope that Gabe had been found after she'd stopped monitoring the transmissions over the radio.

The search team would be gathered by a roaring fire in the hearth in the living room, unwinding, eating hot food, rehashing the details of the long, tedious day.

She would appear as seven kinds of a fool for having come pounding on the door, but she didn't care, as long as Gabe was safe. She would apologize for disturbing him, beat a hasty retreat, and drive away.

Do you know the difference between being alone and being lonely?

Gabe's words once again echoed in Sara's mind, and she nodded.

"Yes, Gabe," she said aloud, staring at the house, "I finally do know the difference, and without you, Gabriel Porter, I'm going to be very, very lonely."

Enough of that, Sara, she admonished herself. She wasn't there as a woman, per se. She'd arrived in the role of a highly trained Search and Rescue expert. She didn't have a gender at the moment, she only had a purpose.

She closed her eyes for a moment, mentally focusing on her inner self, her center, gathering her emotions into a tight bundle directed at nothing other than the mission of finding Gabe. After taking a deep, cleansing breath, she got out of the vehicle and hurried to the front door of the house.

Her knock was answered by Moses, who looked very tired and haggard.

"Hello, Moses," she said quietly.

"Sara," he said, nodding. He stepped back to allow her to enter, then closed the door behind her. "Thought you might show up here."

"I've been monitoring the radio transmissions most of the day at Jeb Broffy's. You didn't find..."

"No," he said, shaking his head. "Gabe is still out there in the Junipers. Somewhere. Come on in and sit by the fire."

When Sara entered the living room with Moses, the other members of the team began to struggle to their feet.

"No, please," she said, raising one hand, "don't get up." Her gaze swept over Chuck, Ben and Billy. "You're all exhausted."

"Yes, ma'am," Billy said.

Moses sank heavily onto an easy chair with a weary sigh. All four men looked at Sara where she remained standing in the center of the room.

"I know that Gabe didn't come back in with you," she said, her voice trembling slightly. "I assume that you'll be going out at first light to search for him."

Moses nodded. "It'll just be us. The Yavapai County Back Country Unit had a call waiting for them at base camp, reporting an overdue hunter over near Prescott. They'll be heading that way at dawn. We're going back to the Junipers for Gabe."

"Moses, all of you," Sara said, "I'm asking if I may go along. I have my equipment with me and... I don't know which of you is Incident Commander now, in Gabe's place, but I'm volunteering to go...if you'll have me."

The four men exchanged glances, sending and receiving messages in a male language that Sara couldn't decipher. She was hardly breathing as she waited for their answer.

"Seems to me," Moses said finally, "that the mission calls for the best trained person we've got to lead it, as long as the person understands that we're not coming back in without Gabe."

"We'll bring him home, Moses," Sara said, hearing the conviction ringing in her voice. "Are you the Incident Commander?"

"No, ma'am," he said, "*you* are."

Sara was so stunned and emotionally moved by the show of confidence from Gabe's team that she was unable to speak.

"The way I see it," Ben said, "I wouldn't want to be the one standing in your way, Sara, once you set out to get ole Gabriel back home where he belongs. A woman hell-bent on finding her man is a mighty force to be reckoned with."

A warm flush stained Sara's cheeks.

Good grief, she thought, it seemed as though the whole world knew she was in love with Gabe before *she* did.

"Besides," Billy said, smiling. "If Moses is busy being Incident Commander, bossing everyone around and all, who's going to fix us hot chocolate out there in those cold Juniper Mountains?"

"Good point," Chuck said. "That settles it then. Sara's the Incident Commander."

"Thank you, all of you...." Sara had to clear her throat as emotions choked off her words. "Get some sleep, gentlemen. We start at dawn, and end at Heaven's Gate."

"Amen," Moses said.

The four men pushed themselves wearily to their feet, fatigue evident in every move they made.

Chuck told Sara that Reggie had been up to the house to inquire about Gabe and would relay the information to the other ranch hands. Rio was a small town, and word would be out by now, Chuck continued, about Gabe being lost in the Junipers.

"If this is our base camp we should have someone on the radio," Sara said.

"I took care of that," Chuck said. "Reggie will be here at dawn. The sheriff is standing by but admits he doesn't have the manpower to help us. Search and Rescue in these parts is all volunteers."

"Yes, I know," Sara said. And at one time she'd stood in very harsh judgment of volunteer units. She'd changed so much since returning to Autumn. No, correct that. She'd grown since Gabriel Porter had come into her life.

"Moses," she said, "do you have a terrain map of the Junipers that I can look at? I haven't been out on a mission all day like you men have, so I'm not ready for bed. It'll save time in the morning if I study the area tonight."

Moses produced the map, along with a transparent plastic overlay that showed the exact route they had taken and how many miles they'd covered before finding the Boy Scouts and their leader. Sara was again extremely impressed with the professionalism of Gabe's team.

The men left. Sara made herself a cup of instant coffee and sat down at the kitchen table to study the map.

Two hours later, she stood and stretched, staring down at the map and overlay sheet.

"Where are you, Gabe?" she said aloud. "What happened to you?"

She narrowed her eyes and frowned as she continued to scrutinize the map, as though willing it to tell her where Gabe was. One thing kept creeping to the front of her mind as she studied the map.

Caves.

The mountain range was dotted with caves, three of which were close enough to where Gabe had last transmitted on the radio to have possibilities as being where he might have sought shelter.

Sara nodded, then glanced at her watch. She hoped she could sleep, because she was going to need every ounce of energy she could muster the next day. The rough terrain of the Junipers made Thinker's Thumb appear like a Sunday picnic.

After rinsing out her cup, she turned off the kitchen light, then wandered back into the living room.

How strange it felt to be there in Gabe's house, making coffee, about to go to bed, acting as though she belonged there and was simply waiting for him to come home... to her.

Don't, Sara, she told herself. Gabe would be coming home because she was going to find him. But he wasn't returning to be with her. She'd lost him before she'd had enough courage to admit to herself that she loved him. What they'd had was over before she'd allowed it to have a chance to really begin. And the pain of that realization would haunt her for the remainder of her days... and nights.

Sara sighed, then made a quick trip to her vehicle for a few items she needed to spend the night. She found blankets and a pillow in a closet, added logs to the fire, then prepared for bed.

She'd sleep on the sofa in front of the fireplace, she decided. Using one of Gabe's guest bedrooms while knowing he wasn't in the big bed in his room was more than she could emotionally handle. Gabe was spending the night in the dark and dangerous Juniper Mountains while she was warm and safe in his house. But tomorrow night, by damn, he'd be home at Heaven's Gate where he belonged.

To Sara's amazement and relief, she slept soundly, waking early and feeling well rested. She showered, dressed and had a pot of coffee brewing when the others arrived at dawn's light. Reggie came in the back door as Moses, Billy, Ben and Chuck came in the front.

Reggie disappeared into Gabe's den to check out the radio and tune into the frequency Moses had given to match the radio in Chuck's vehicle.

With coffee mugs in hand, the four men stood around the kitchen table as Sara briefed them on how she wanted to handle the mission.

"Any questions?" she said finally.

"Well," Moses said, "it works for me...sort of. We'll do a Zigzag Line Search. Billy and I will head for Cave One, Chuck and Ben to Two."

"Right," Sara said.

"That's where the 'sort of' comes in," Moses said, looking at her. "That leaves you on your own moving toward the third cave. The lay of the land in that sector will make it impossible for us to see each other. Nope. Not good."

"I realize I'll be alone, Moses," she said, "but the weather is clear and radio transmission should be fine. I'll keep in touch with all of you in fifteen-minute intervals. As the Incident Commander, I take the extra risks if the need arises. So be it."

There was that word again, she thought. *Risks.*

Moses stroked his chin. "I don't like it."

"Too late," she said breezily, beginning to roll up the map and overlay. "I'm in charge of the team, you're in charge of hot chocolate. Saddle up, cowpokes."

"Lordy," Moses said, "Gabe surely does have his hands full dealing with this little lady."

The other men hooted with laughter, Sara blushed and ignored them.

The air was biting cold due to the lack of cloud cover. Sara drove her vehicle, following Chuck, Billy having elected to ride with Sara. The youngest member of the team talked nonstop about food, even to the point of repeating exact recipes for some of his favorite dishes.

Sara smiled inwardly, remembering the drive to Thinker's Thumb when Gabe had chatted away, trying to get her to relax to obtain a proper balance of emotion regarding the mission ahead.

"That sounds delicious, Billy," she said. "What would you serve with it?"

"Well, now," he said, "I'm glad you asked. You gotta have homemade bread straight from the oven. Yes, ma'am, hot homemade bread. Then you put a pot of dairy butter on the table and..."

Oh, yes, Sara thought, as Billy continued with the menu, Gabriel Porter had trained his men very, very well.

They drove as far into the Juniper Mountain range as was possible, parked the vehicles, then put on their outerwear. Sara handed them the plastic marking tape. Before Chuck locked his vehicle, he made radio contact with Reggie.

"There's a storm coming in fast," Reggie said. "I've got Gabe's weather radio tuned in beside me here, and just heard the bulletin. It's approaching from behind the Junipers, and is carrying a mighty heavy load of snow. Over."

Sara and the others were standing by the open door of Chuck's vehicle, and everyone scanned the sky.

"Can't see anything yet, Reggie," Chuck said, "but thanks for the warning. Over."

"You guys better trek fast out there," Reggie said. "I figure Gabe's had enough of having his butt frozen. Oh, excuse me, Miss Calhoun. I'm outta here. I mean, over and out."

"I imagine Reggie's right about Gabe and his frozen butt," Sara said. "Gentlemen, let's do it."

Two hours later, Sara hunkered down and leaned her back against a tall pine tree. She closed her eyes for a moment, focusing on her remaining inner energy and fighting her fatigue.

The snow on the ground was wet and heavy, making the climb slow and difficult. Her leg muscles ached with a burning pain, and she was at least another hour away from the cave she was headed for.

The last radio contact she'd had with the two pairs of men had confirmed that they weren't able to move any faster than she was.

The sky was darkening. The storm Reggie had warned them about was moving across the heavens like a curtain being pulled into place, accompanied by a bone-chilling wind.

While Sara knew that each of them was thinking it, no one had asked the dreaded question aloud—what would they do if Gabe wasn't in one of the three caves?

"Dear God," she said, shaking her head.

She forced herself to her feet and started slowly off again.

Gabe *had* to be in one of the caves, her mind hammered. He just had to be. If he'd lost his way in the whiteout and stayed put in his tent for the night, he would have started back down the mountain by now, met up with them, and they'd all be together, drinking Moses's hot chocolate.

That he had been hurt was now a near certainty. If he'd sought shelter in a cave, he would have left it at dawn's light if he'd been able.

Yes, he was injured.

How badly?

Where was he?

And the nightmare question—what would they do if he wasn't in one of the caves?

Fifteen minutes later, snow began to fall in big, wet flakes, slowly at first, then increasing. With it came a howling wind that whipped the snow into a frenzy.

Flashes of fear swept through Sara as she trudged on, remembering her panic when she'd been enclosed within the walls of white on Thinker's Thumb, and the dreams she'd had of being so cold and alone in a snow storm. She shoved the tormenting memories to the back of her mind, praying they'd stay there.

"Heaven One, this is Heaven Three. Over," came a static-filled transmission over her radio.

"This is Heaven One. What do you have, Moses? Over."

"Cave One is empty. No sign of anyone having been here. Over."

Oh, God, Sara thought.

"All right, Heaven Three, take cover in the cave and rest. Keep near the entrance so you can pick up radio transmissions. If this storm goes to whiteout, stay put inside until it's clear again. Over," Sara ordered.

"Roger. Over and out."

And Sara moved on.

Twenty minutes later, to Sara's horror, the crackling radio delivered a carbon copy of Moses's message. Chuck reported that Gabe was not in Cave Two. With a sinking heart, she gave Chuck and Ben the same instructions she'd issued to Moses and Billy.

And Sara moved on.

Now she could hardly see more than a few feet in front of her, and used her compass to stay on track. She could taste the metallic flavor of fear in her mouth and ignored it. The snow increased its velocity even more.

Just a few more yards, she told herself, pushing one foot in front of the other. Just a few more...just a few more...just a few more.

The entrance to the cave seemed to appear out of nowhere in the blinding snow, like a giant, dark mouth waiting to gobble her up.

She was so startled that she lost her footing and fell flat on her stomach. The momentum of her fall onto the wet snow propelled her forward into the cave as though riding tummy down on a sled.

She came to an abrupt halt as she hit the dry ground inside and gasped for breath as she lifted her head.

"Hello, Sara Ann," Gabe said, grinning at her. "To quote ole Hux, what took you so long?"

Chapter Nineteen

Sara blinked, then decided in the next instant that when she'd executed her less-than-graceful belly flop, she'd cut off the oxygen to her brain and was hallucinating.

"Sara?" Gabe said, his smile changing into a frown. "Are you all right?"

Dear Lord, she thought, it was really Gabe. She'd found him, alive, breathing. Oh, Gabriel.

She scrambled to her feet and hurried across the three yards separating them, dropping to her knees beside him where he sat propped against the wall, a survival blanket draped over him.

"Gabe?" she whispered, her eyes darting over every inch of his magnificent face before meeting his gaze.

She lifted one hand as though to touch him, then dropped it back onto her knee. "Thank God. We were all so worried about you."

"I—"

"We," she said, stiffening. She reached for the walkie-talkie clipped to her belt. "I've got to tell Moses, Chuck, Ben, Billy that you're okay."

The radio produced nothing but static. Sara got to her feet again and went to the entrance of the cave, hoping for a clear transmission.

"Nothing," she said. "Darn, it's really wild out there. I'll just have to wait until this storm passes through enough to radio, and to allow us to get out of here."

"It's just like old times," Gabe said quietly. "Reminds me of when we were in my tent on Thinker's Thumb."

Sara moved away from the chill at the entrance and sat down Indian-style beside Gabe. Their eyes met and held. She was aware of the increased tempo of her heart and the threat of burning tears in her eyes.

Gabe was alive, her mind sang. Oh, how she loved him, wanted to fling herself into his arms and feel his strength, the solid power of his body. She wanted to touch him from head to toe to reassure herself that he was really there, safe and well.

"You'd better take off your outerwear," Gabe said, breaking the sensuous spell weaving around them. "It's plenty warm in here."

"Yes, of course."

She fussed busily with the snaps, lecturing herself the whole time to calm down, get it together, not leap into Gabe's lap. She unzipped her jacket, revealing a heavy red flannel shirt she wore tucked into black quilt-lined corduroy pants.

"So," she said, striving for a run-of-the-mill, pleasant tone of voice. "What happened to you?"

"I fell on my head," he said dryly, "like a rookie team member. It was *not* a class act. I tried to move around in a whiteout condition, like an idiot, fell and knocked myself out cold. Luckily, I wasn't unconscious long, or I wouldn't be here to talk about it. I knew there were caves up here, so when I managed to stumble into this one, I was one grateful son of a gun, believe me."

Keep talking, Porter, he ordered himself. What he *wanted* to do was haul Sara into his arms and kiss her senseless. He'd known, he'd just somehow known, that she'd join up with the rest of his team and come looking for him. And there she was, so beautiful, so enticing, and he loved her so damn much.

"I broke my radio when I fell," he went on. "I figured I had a slight concussion so I built a small fire in here with the duff the wind had blown in over time, with the idea that having to tend to the fire would help keep me awake."

"That's good," she said, nodding. "A person shouldn't sleep more than a half hour to forty-five minutes at a time when there's any chance of a concussion. But why didn't you start down the mountain at dawn? Surely you know that I... that your team would be looking for you."

"I pulled another rookie stunt," he said with a snort of self-disgust. "I fell asleep just before dawn, and missed my chance to leave the cave. When I woke up, it was bad outside again, and I was stuck. It was snowing too hard for a signal flare to be seen. Damn. I've been plenty warm enough with my sleeping bag and survival blanket, but I'm mad as hell at myself for screwing up."

"You didn't carry that fancy tent of yours?"

"Not this time. The Junipers are rough going, so I lightened my pack some. Do you know that professional climbers drill holes in the handles of their toothbrushes to make them weigh less? Every fraction of an ounce is vitally important to them. That fascinates me."

"Yes, it's... it's very interesting. How does your head feel now?"

"I have a headache, but I'm not dizzy, and my vision is clear. I'm fine, except for my pride."

"I'm glad you're all right, Gabe," she said softly.

He looked directly into her eyes. "Thank you, and thank you, too, for coming out to rescue me." He shook his head. "I hope Moses didn't call for a mission number this morning. To have an official report written up on the search for, then rescue of, team leader Gabriel Porter, would be embarrassing as hell."

"*I'm* the Incident Commander and, no, I didn't take the time to get a mission number."

"My team appointed you Incident Commander?"

"Yes," she said, lifting her chin. "They did."

"Smart boys. You're one of the best I've seen in Search and Rescue work, Sara."

She pulled a rolled package from her pack, and opened it to reveal a blue, puffy, down sleeping bag. Like Gabe, she removed her boots and set them next to the small fire he'd made that was still glowing.

"Yes, I'm very good at Search and Rescue," she said, moving to sit cross-legged on the sleeping bag. "I'm prepared to take all the risks involved to be excellent in that arena." She busied herself smoothing out the sleeping bag around her, keeping her eyes averted from Gabe's.

"Sara," he said, his voice very low, "I owe you an apology."

"Oh?" she said, still not looking at him.

"I've had a lot of time to think while I've been up here, and I realize that I've done you a great injustice."

Sara's head snapped up, and she looked at him questioningly. He met her gaze.

"*I* decided," he said, "with arrogance, what was best for you, how you should be conducting your life. Changing *my* life-style from the fast-lane, career-oriented routine, to the one that included stopping to smell the flowers, having a better balance was, decreed know-it-all Porter, what *you* should do."

"Gabe..."

"I don't know who in the hell I thought I was," he said, as though she hadn't spoken. "While I was on my quest to save you from yourself, I fell in love with you, Sara Ann. Then when you didn't salute, snap to, follow my orders regarding your life-style, I became angry and was very hurt.

"Sara, I'm sorry. I was so damn wrong. I tried to change you, without even considering the fact that you might be perfectly happy just as you were. What's right for me, I now realize, isn't necessarily right for you. I do love you, but that's mine to deal with. I truly apologize for the hateful things I said to you. You've set your goals for your future, and I hope you accomplish every one of them.

"I hope you'll forgive me, Sara, for any pain I caused you by saying the rotten things to you that I did. I'll stay out of your life, only see you when we have a Search and Rescue mission to tackle together, but could you find it in your heart to forgive me for being such a jerk?"

"No."

He closed his eyes and leaned his head back against the wall of the cave.

"Hell," he said, then sighed. He opened his eyes again and looked at her. "Well, the way I treated you, I don't really deserve to be forgiven. I'll have to live with that."

"Gabe, no, you don't understand," she said, her voice trembling. "You turned my life upside down from the moment I met you, confusing me, causing me to experience emotions that were new, foreign to me.

"When Doc Hartman told me the truth about my father's death, my confusion increased tenfold. I didn't know who I was, what I was really supposed to be doing with my life. I was lost, and terribly frightened."

"I know," he said. "I held you the night it all came crashing down on you. But then you regrouped, and it was business as usual. When you said you were going to start the junior Search and Rescue team with the Huxley boys and their friends, I knew I was beat. I knew I'd lost you, Sara."

Tears filled her eyes, and she attempted unsuccessfully to blink them away.

"No, Gabe, you didn't lose me. *I* was lost within my own maze of fear and confusion. But when you didn't come back from the mission up here, when I'd sat for hours at Martha's and Jeb's, monitoring the radio transmissions, hoping, praying, for your safety, I..."

Two tears slid unnoticed down her cheeks.

"I knew, Gabe, that..." A sob caught in her throat. "I love you so much."

Every muscle in Gabe's body tensed and his heart began to beat a wild tattoo. His gaze was riveted on Sara's pale, tear-streaked face, and he nearly forgot to breathe.

"And, Gabe? I *do* know the difference between being alone and being lonely now. Without you in my life, I will be very, *very* lonely. *I'm* the one who's sorry, who's asking that *you* forgive *me*. I was such a child, so afraid to run the risks of loving, just as you accused me of."

She dashed the tears from her cheeks, but more spilled over.

"I've been fully prepared," she went on, "to take the risks connected to Search and Rescue work, and now I'm ready to put the past behind me and move forward, running the risks of loving. Loving you, Gabe, only you."

"Sara, I—"

"Wait, please," she said, "let me finish. I'm not entering the election for sheriff. Being a deputy is just fine. I'm not going to attempt to start a Search and Rescue unit of my own, either. I'll be a member of your team if you'll have me. I want to teach the teenagers, start the junior unit, because they're the teams of the future, and it's a positive and worthwhile project. Gabe, I brought something with me in the hope that it would be tangible, visible proof to you of the truth of all I'm saying."

With shaking hands, Sara unbuttoned the pocket of the flannel shirt and withdrew something Gabe couldn't see clearly until she extended it toward him.

It was the tiny bunch of silk lily of the valley flowers from the sash on Rosalie's dress.

"Flowers," she said, hardly above a whisper. "Flowers, Gabe, to let you know that I will gladly, joyfully, stop and smell the flowers with you for the rest of my life. I love you, Gabriel Porter, with all that I am."

"Sara," he said, his voice choked with tears as he accepted the flowers. "Ah, Sara." He held out his arms to her. "Come here."

And she went.

She moved onto his lap, wrapping her arms around his neck and gazing at him, tears glistening in his dark eyes and her green eyes, love shining in both.

"I love you, Sara Ann. Will you marry me? Please?"

She smiled. "Will you give me Snazzy the kitten as my wedding present?"

He carefully placed the silk flowers back in her pocket.

"You'll have Snazzy complete with a red bow on her head."

"Then, yes, I'll marry you."

Gabe laughed, but in the next instant, his mouth claimed hers, his tongue delving deep inside.

Passion exploded within them, consuming them, leaving no room for any shadows of confusion, pain, doubts, that may have lingered. They were in love, and loved in kind, and the tomorrows were theirs to share for eternity.

"I want to make love to you, Sara," Gabe said, when he finally ended the searing kiss.

"But your head..."

He chuckled. "Do you want me to say, 'Not now, dear, I have a headache'? My head is fine. Make love with me, Sara Ann, here, in another one of our private worlds."

"Yes."

They spread out the sleeping bags, making a puffy bed as soft as a cloud. While Gabe placed more duff on the fire, Sara took a candle lantern from her pack. It was four inches high and three inches across. She lit the candle, drew up a glass cylinder that was inside the metal casing to produce an eight-inch lantern. Despite its small size, its special design caused it to cast a glow over a large area of the cave.

"Oh, Gabe, look," she said, awe evident in her voice.

He followed her gaze and his eyes widened. The candlelight was making the flecks of mica in the walls and ceiling of the cave glitter like sparkling diamonds. The sight was spectacularly beautiful.

"Incredible," Gabe said, his gaze sweeping over the ceiling and walls. He looked at Sara. "I'll never forget this moment, or that I shared it with you. You're my life, Sara, and very soon you'll be my wife."

"I love you, Gabe."

They shed their clothes quickly, then reached for each other as they lay on the soft bedding.

They kissed until their rough breathing echoed in their private cocoon of paradise, then Gabe moved to pay homage to the bounty of each of Sara's breasts in turn.

Sara's hands caressed his taut, strong body, rediscovering all that he was, rejoicing in what his masculinity would bring to the heated haven of her femininity.

Lips followed hands, nibbling, teasing, tasting, heightening their passions to a heated flame that was hotter than the small fire burning near them. Their bodies glistened, then mirrored the millions of diamondlike images dancing from the sparkling mica.

Another world, their world.

It was ecstasy.

It was beauty beyond the scope of imagination. It was two bodies meshed into one entity, sealing a commitment of forever, together.

They made love, the rhythm perfectly matched, sending them closer and closer to what they sought, then flinging them, moments apart, up and beyond the glittering sky of their glorious world.

"Gabe!"

"Sara. Sara Ann!"

They floated slowly back, sated, happiness a nearly palpable entity. Gabe moved off Sara, then drew her close to his side, flipping the free section of the sleeping bag over their cooling bodies.

Quietly, lazily, so contented, they talked, making plans for the future.

Children? Oh, yes, two, maybe three. The ranch would be a wonderful place to raise a family. Maybe Sara should consider being a deputy in Rio, to save herself the drive to Autumn. That had possibilities. The empty bunkhouse? It could be used for the camp for the junior Search and Rescue Unit, but no curtains on the windows, absolutely none. Rosalie, someday, would be given to their daughter, but the tiny silk lily of the valley flowers were Gabe's.

It was pillow talk, secrets, the major and mundane, and the most wondrous part was that they knew it could all come true.

Finally, reluctantly, they reached for their clothes as they realized that the wind that had howled outside was rapidly decreasing.

They'd just finished dousing the fire and replacing their gear when Sara's radio squawked.

"Heaven One, this is Heaven Three. Can you hear me? Blasted static. Heaven One, are you reading me at all? Over."

Sara picked up the radio and smiled as she handed it to Gabe.

"Heaven Three," Gabe said into the device, "you shouldn't be saying things like 'blasted static' over the airwaves. Over."

"Gabe?" Moses answered. "Heaven Two, you hearing this? Gabe's on the radio. Over."

"This is Heaven Two. Good to hear your voice, Gabe. You're a helluva lot of trouble, buddy, but I guess you're worth it. Over."

"Gabe, Moses here. I sure hope you've got Sara with you 'cause I don't hear her talking back and forth with us. Over."

"She's right here with me, Moses," Gabe said. "We'll meet you guys at the bottom of the mountain, then head on home. Over."

"Roger. Where are you now, Gabe? Over."

Gabe dropped a quick kiss on Sara's lips, then said, "Miss Sara Ann Calhoun and I are at Heaven's Gate. Over and out."

* * * * *

Dark secrets, dangerous desire...

Lovers DARK AND DANGEROUS

Three spine-tingling tales from the dark side of love.

This October, enter the world of shadowy romance as Silhouette presents the third in their annual tradition of thrilling love stories and chilling story lines. Written by three of Silhouette's top names:

LINDSAY McKENNA
LEE KARR
RACHEL LEE

Haunting a store near you this October.

Only from

Silhouette®

...where passion lives.

LDD

Silhouette ROMANCE™

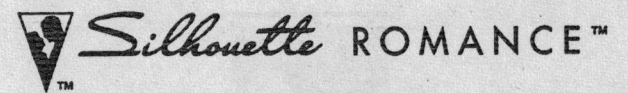

First comes marriage.... Will love follow?
Find out this September when Silhouette Romance presents

Hasty Weddings

Join six couples who marry for convenient reasons, and still find happily-ever-afters. Look for these wonderful books by some of your favorite authors:

#1030 *Timely Matrimony* by Kasey Michaels
#1031 *McCullough's Bride* by Anne Peters
#1032 *One of a Kind Marriage* by Cathie Linz
#1033 *Oh, Baby!* by Lauryn Chandler
#1034 *Temporary Groom* by Jayne Addison
#1035 *Wife in Name Only* by Carolyn Zane

HASTY

MIRA™

The brightest star in women's fiction!

This October, reach for the stars and watch all your dreams come true with **MIRA BOOKS**.

HEATHER GRAHAM POZZESSERE
Slow Burn in October
An enthralling tale of murder and passion set against the dark and glittering world of Miami.

SANDRA BROWN
The Devil's Own in November
She made a deal with the devil...but she didn't bargain on losing her heart.

BARBARA BRETTON
Tomorrow & Always in November
Unlikely lovers from very different worlds... They had to cross time to find one another.

PENNY JORDAN
For Better For Worse in December
Three couples, three dreams—can they rekindle the love and passion that first brought them together?

The sky has no limit with **MIRA BOOKS**.

STT-R

Silhouette SPECIAL EDITION

THE Jones GANG

by Christine Rimmer

Three rapscallion brothers. Their main talent: making trouble. Their only hope: three uncommon women who knew the way to heal a wounded heart! Meet them in these books:

Jared Jones

hadn't had it easy with women. Retreating to his mountain cabin, he found willful Eden Parker waiting to show him a good woman's love in MAN OF THE MOUNTAIN (May, SE #886).

Patrick Jones

was determined to show Regina Black that a wild Jones boy was *not* husband material. But that wouldn't stop her from trying to nab him in SWEETBRIAR SUMMIT (July, SE #896)!

Jack Roper

came to town looking for the wayward and beautiful Olivia Larrabee. He never suspected he'd uncover a long-buried Jones family secret in A HOME FOR THE HUNTER (September, SE #908)....

Meet these rascal men and the women who'll tame them, only from Silhouette Books and Special Edition!

If you missed either of the first two books in THE JONES GANG series, *Man of the Mountain* (SE #886), or *Sweetbriar Summit* (SE #896), order your copy now by sending your name, address, zip or postal code along with a check or money order (please do not send cash) for $3.50 ($3.99 in Canada for SE #896) plus 75¢ postage and handling ($1.00 in Canada), payable to Silhouette Books, to:

In the U.S.	In Canada
Silhouette Books	Silhouette Books
3010 Walden Ave.	P. O. Box 636
P. O. Box 9077	Fort Erie, Ontario
Buffalo, NY 14269-9077	L2A 5X3

Please specify book title(s) with order.
Canadian residents add applicable federal and provincial taxes.

JONESF

Silhouette SPECIAL EDITION

Open these Love Letters from Lisa Jackson...

A IS FOR ALWAYS (October, SE #914)

Years ago, dark family secrets tore young lovers Max McKee and Skye Donahue apart. Now, their unending desire would no longer be denied—but could those demons of the past still keep them apart?

B IS FOR BABY (November, SE #920)

In a single passionate night with Jenner McKee, Beth Crandall's life changed forever. Now, years later, she had returned home to tell the man she'd never stopped loving that he was a father!

C IS FOR COWBOY (December, SE #926)

Mysterious forces stalked Casey McKee's powerful family, suddenly making her a target. Only brooding cowboy Sloan Redhawk could save her—and only Casey could make this loner's passion stir anew!

Watch for Lisa Jackson's new series, **LOVE LETTERS**, beginning in October with A IS FOR ALWAYS—only from Silhouette Special Edition!

Sometimes all it takes is a letter of love to rebuild dreams of the past....

LOVE1